Meet the employees of
Deadly Force, Inc.

Luke Simpson: Founder and president. Vietnam Vet, ex-cop, former CIA, he got tired of playing by the rules. Now, this deadly soldier of fortune picks the job—and calls the shots.

Jake O'Bannion: Management and services. This hard-nosed ex-New York City cop is the caretaker of Deadly Force's HQ on Superstition Mountain. And his fighting skills are more than lethal.

Ben Sanchez: Warrior-for-hire. He fought with the Rangers in 'Nam. Now, this silent Apache is a part-time mercenary—and one of the deadliest on Simpson's team.

Tran Cao: Science and technology. Toughened by the war in his homeland, this sharp-witted South Vietnamese can master the world's most advanced computers—and most devastating weapons.

Calvin Steeples: Chief pilot. He was a flier in Nam. Now, he's a cropduster—when he's not helping Simpson destroy more dangerous vermin.

Deadly Force

The DEADLY FORCE Series
published by Berkley Books

DEADLY FORCE
SPECIAL DELIVERY

DEADLY FORCE

Special Delivery

Mark Dixon

BERKLEY BOOKS, NEW YORK

This is a work of fiction. The characters, incidents, places and dialogues are products of the author's imagination and are not to be construed as real. The author's use of names of actual persons, living or dead, is incidental to the purposes of the plot and is not intended to change the entirely fictional character of the work.

DEADLY FORCE: SPECIAL DELIVERY

A Berkley Book / published by arrangement with
the author

PRINTING HISTORY
Berkley edition/November 1987

ISBN: 0-425-10479-6

A BERKLEY BOOK® TM 757,375
Berkley Books are published by The Berkley Publishing Group,
200 Madison Avenue, New York, NY 10016.
The name "BERKLEY" and the "B" logo
are trademarks belonging to Berkley Publishing Corporation.

PRINTED IN THE UNITED STATES OF AMERICA

10 9 8 7 6 5 4 3 2 1

CHAPTER 1

The countdown was proceeding according to expectations.

The sun was still an hour away when Major Gregor Schevardnadze stepped out into the cold. Two thousand meters away, a column of shadow stood against the dark gray sky. The gantry had been rolled into place seventy-two hours before.

In less than three hours the gargantuan SL-13 would begin to thunder. The largest rocket in the Soviet arsenal, its engines would belch fire, shaking the ground for a dozen kilometers. Then, like a roman candle, it would be gone, a trail of smoke the only evidence it had ever been there.

The rocket was an old familiar, in use since 1968. Its failures had been few and closely examined. It dwarfed the SL-3 that had carried Gagarin into orbit and carried three times the payload.

The gray sky was familiar too. He'd been here at Plesetsk off and on for seventeen years, seen it grow from a sleepy, bog-ridden backwater to become the busiest spaceport on earth. Eight hundred kilometers north of Moscow, it was perfect for putting satellites in polar orbit. And an ideal location for approaching U.S. territory across the Pole.

1

That proximity was a blessing and a curse. The weather was unpredictable and harsh. Much of the year, Plesetsk was buried in snow, and during the short summers mosquitoes swarmed out of the bogs in clouds, capable of blanketing an unprotected arm in seconds, leaving a bloated, welt-covered wreck behind.

Schevardnadze had seen more than four thousand launches, been launch supervisor for a third of them, and still he had never seen anything like this one.

The first indication that something unusual was going on was the herd of GRU and KGB types descending on the cosmodrome. Like rooting pigs, they turned the place upside down, asking hundreds of questions and answering none. When they were satisfied, or at least content to allow matters to proceed, their numbers had been reduced—no longer a herd but still an annoying distraction.

That was when the real work had begun. An SL-13 had been stripped down, its fuel capacity expanded by the addition of three extra tanks, arrayed in a circle against the rocket's outer skin to distribute the extra weight evenly. The several tons of extra fuel could mean only one thing—a heavy payload, even heavier than the Mir space station launched earlier that year.

He wondered what it was all about and knew there was no point in asking. If they wanted him to know, they would tell him. That was the Soviet way. So thick was the cloak of secrecy that for the first time in his experience the launch tower was dark. The usual blur of work lights and stabbing search beams was absent.

The major lit an American cigarette, cupping the feeble flame of his engraved lighter in a mittened fist. The snow on the ground crunched as he shuffled his feet, and he was aware for the first time of just how cold it was. Inside, the windowless control room was a uniform twenty degrees Celsius, maintained by elaborate climate-control equipment to prevent overheating of the massive array of electronic gear controlling the launch.

He puffed nervously on the cigarette. The Marlboros were a cosmopolitan affectation wryly tolerated by his colleagues, none of whom smoked. He knew he should give up the habit, but until he could, at least he'd smoke something that tasted half decent. He dragged the cigarette down to the filter, then tossed it to the snow, crushing it under the toe of his arctic boot.

November was a hell of a time for a special launch, but today, the seventeenth, had particular significance in Soviet history. Maybe the payload really was something unusual. Not too likely, but one never knew.

The sky was considerably brighter than when he'd first stepped outside, but the solid gray overcast showed no sign of breaking up. The gantry was more clearly defined now, individual struts and columns jumping out of the darker bulk. A thin plume of steam coiled lazily skyward from the launchpad, only to be torn to rags by brisk winds before it had climbed halfway up the length of the rocket.

Schevardnadze shook his head at the futility of it all, then turned and tugged at the heavy stainless-steel door to launch control. Back inside, his glasses fogged over. He dropped them carelessly on the steel desk by the door while he shrugged out of his parka. He wiped the glasses clean, then put them back on, walking back to his elevated swivel chair, partially blinded by half-moons of moisture condensing on the lower lenses of his bifocals.

Resuming his seat, the private uncertainty dissipated as quickly as it had come. Doubt was something best reserved for oneself, preferably confined to moments of solitude. Glancing at the countdown clock on the main control panel, he knew he wouldn't be alone again until after lift-off.

It was 2:47:32:00 and counting.

He watched the clock unravel back toward zero for a moment, then turned to his assistant.

"So far, so good, eh, Lieutenant?"

The younger man gave him a quizzical look, as if to ask why he should even have to inquire. Schevardnadze smiled, giving his earnest young comrade the thumbs-up. The clock rolled inexorably backward, and Schevardnadze wondered if zero hour meant the dawn of a new age or the end of time.

• • •

The seconds ticked off in hundredths.

The mesmerizing glitter of red and green lights winking and flashing caught Schevardnadze's attention now and then. Somehow their hypnotic allure distracted him just enough from the monotony. The mutter of voices, the cramped quarters, and the inevitable tension as lift-off approached were the worst part of the job. *Anxiety* was too tame a word: insanity suggested too much disorder. Ultimately there was no way to explain such a time.

"Thirty seconds . . ."

The squawk box fractured his reverie, and for the first time in more than an hour he became aware of his hands. They had been proceeding by rote, moving through the complicated routine on autopilot. He had done it so often, he could have done it blindfolded. In a way, he realized, that's exactly what he had done.

"Twenty . . ."

But now he had to be alert. Having come this far, the decision was now his, and his alone. Whether to go or not was up to him. It made no difference that he had no idea what dark secret lay swaddled in the nose cone of the mammoth SL-13. He was in command now; he was like God . . . or Lenin.

"Ten . . ."

Schevardnadze watched the array of monitors. All systems were go. Everything was normal. The ground had begun its familiar shuddering as the rocket engines approached full thrust. Outside, he knew, the air was full of thunder, the gantry nearly obscured by smoke and clouds of steam. His feet trembled on the floor, his coffee lapped at the brim of its cup, dark mocha circles, wave upon wave, trying to escape their prison.

"Five . . . four . . . three . . ."

And it was now or never. His eyes danced from meter to gauge, then, with what came as close to prayer as anything he'd ever uttered, Schevardnadze pressed the penultimate button. In his mind's eye he saw the tower fall away, its halves crashing back against their hydraulic brakes and bouncing spasmodically.

"Two . . ."

The final button felt hot under his thumb. He pressed it and felt nothing. So simple, it all seemed so simple. And the final cables dangled now. Cut loose by his signal, they waved frantically, like severed umbilicals, coiling downward reluctantly, straining to maintain contact, a control no longer theirs.

"One . . ."

Rising thunder filled the concrete-and-steel bunker, and Schevardnadze's teeth rattled. The greedy engines, gorged on fuel and demanding still more, pushed against the earth. He turned to a large TV monitor on the wall above him. The thunder made thought all but impossible.

And he knew, even before he understood, that something was dreadfully wrong.

The smoke pouring from the rocket boosters was too thick, too dark, like night itself pouring from the motors. The rocket yawed crazily, less than a kilometer off the ground, then tipped awkwardly, as if it had tripped over something no one could see.

Then it was gone, swallowed by the overcast.

A low rumble swelled through the control room as the technicians began to react. Without turning around he knew by the sound of scraping chairs that many of them had risen, not knowing what else to do. Schevardnadze, nearly numb, reached dumbly for the PA microphone switch on his headset. His fingers fiddled with the toggle. Then, knowing delay would only compound the problem, he clicked it on.

"We have an emergency situation. Code blue. Please remain at your stations and keep silent."

He tore his eyes away from the monitor screen, now gray from edge to edge. There was nothing more to be seen. It all came down now to electronics.

He punched a sequence of buttons on the numeric keypad at his elbow. The screen wavered, then filled with a map of the surrounding area. A wavy streak of light traced the runaway's trajectory. It had nearly reached the edge of the screen already. He punched another set of numbers, and the grid contracted, losing detail but gaining scope.

Over the PA, the tracking detail droned its interminable detail: "Altitude, ten thousand meters, range thirty kilometers. Altitude, twelve thousand meters, range forty kilometers. Altitude, fourteen thousand . . ."

So far, at least the tracking monitors were still functioning. Schevardnadze barked a series of commands into his mike and was rewarded by the return of silence to the control room. Only the intermittent beep of the trackers broke the stillness. He was so absorbed in his duties, he failed to hear the hollow boom of the control-room door thrown open.

Angrily he brushed away the hand on his shoulder, working feverishly to track the errant missile.

"Major Schevardnadze . . ." He was only dimly aware of the repeated shout, like a full-bore mantra bellowed in his ear. The hand returned and shook him roughly, shattering the icy concentration enough for him to realize the nuisance was General Alexander Gribanov.

"Major, what the hell is happening?"

Ignoring etiquette and regulations, Schevardnadze neither stood nor saluted. "I don't know, General. The rocket's out of control."

"It can't be, do you hear me? It can't be."

"Begging your pardon, General, but it is."

"Major, do you have any idea what's on board that rocket?" '

"No, sir, I don't."

"Well, you have to get that damn thing back down here, Major. Now."

"That's out of the question, General. The best we can hope for is to destroy it. It's nearly over the Arctic Ocean. In another ninety seconds it will be. Then we'll blow it."

"You will not, Major. Do you understand me, you will not destroy that rocket. Not without my permission."

"But, General, it's heading toward foreign soil. We can't—"

"You heard what I said, Major. Now, I want you to project earthfall for that rocket. Use all available data. Correct and update whenever necessary."

"General, you can't predict where it will land. It's out of control. Projections are based on predictable flight data. This thing's a rogue. We don't know where it's going to land. My God, General, it's . . ."

But Gribanov was not listening. The general's adjutant was leading him out of the control room. In a second he reappeared behind the tinted glass of the communications room. He was talking animatedly, no doubt explaining events to someone in the Kremlin. The general was waving his free hand wildly, while his features remained rigid. You have to hand it to him, Schevardnadze thought, he is remarkably cool, under the circumstances. And even as Schevardnadze smiled a thin, tight-lipped smile, circumstances suddenly got much worse.

The thin white trace on the monitor stopped growing. The rocket was no longer in contact with Plesetsk.

"Captain Plekhanov?"

"Radio contact broken, Major."

"Why?"

"I don't know, Major."

"Very well. Contact Baikonur. I want everything you can get me from Rorsat monitoring."

"Yes, sir."

Schevardnadze grimaced at the verbal salute.

"Lieutenant Gazenko."

"Yes, sir."

"Report!"

The young woman gulped audibly into her mike before responding. "Nothing to report, Major. Telemetry discontinued at launch plus 9:22:04. No prior warning. I can't say anything more until we get the remote telemetry reports. That will take a few hours."

"Get it sooner, Lieutenant."

"I'll try, sir."

"Don't try, dammit, do it!"

Schevardnadze, his sense of futility mounting, ran down the checklist one by one. There had been no warning. Even after the visual indications were evident, electronic monitoring had revealed nothing. Not, that is, to the naked eye. Of course, the mountains of data from Rorsats and tracking stations around the globe would tell them everything. Everything, that is, except what actually had happened. They might never know that.

Ironically the United States, with its own sophisticated satellites, would probably know almost as much as they did. Maybe more, if their technology was as good as it was cracked up to be. They'd know everything except what was so special about the SL-13's payload. And even he didn't know that. He wondered whether even the general knew.

But right now he had a bigger problem. Old lucky Gregor, he was going to have to break the news to General Gribanov. Whatever it was, they had lost it. Exactly where might take days to figure out.

If it could be done at all.

CHAPTER 2

Like the webs of competing spiders, the electronic intelligence networks of the National Security Agency, NORAD, SAC, and NASA tracked the wild arc of the SL-13. Klaxons blared in a hundred bunkers. Men who seldom saw the light of day rubbed blip-bleared eyes and looked again. Their screens all wore the fuzzy track of the runaway rocket.

A routine watch had become an exercise in doomsday maneuvers. Soviet tests were a dime a dozen. And like most standard launches, the initial appearance of this one was greeted with yawns. Nobody bothered to comment on yet another million-dollar toy tossed into the air like a baby in a blanket.

But when things came unglued, from Australia to Alaska, men scrambled with a fever they hoped would never come. IMEWS and Vela satellites in a dozen orbits shared echoed data, elint transceivers worked overtime. In Colorado, asleep under a billion tons of solid granite, General Arthur Collins felt the hand on his shoulder. His first instinct, consistent with his dream, was to stroke the fingers gently. But even half asleep, he knew something was wrong.

Collins sat up, conscious of a distant alarm. Lieutenant

Adam Kowalski saluted smartly. "General Collins, we've got something big."

"What is it, Lieutenant? Another NASA screwup?" Collins bent over to tie his shoes.

"No, sir, it's the Russkies."

Collins, reaching for his uniform jacket, arrested his hand in midair. "Come again?"

"A Soviet launch, General. An SL-13. That's all I know. Colonel Meyers sent me to get you."

"An SL-13? Is the colonel sure?"

"Yes, sir."

"Christ almighty. I hope to God . . ." Collins didn't finish. He didn't have to. Kowalski, like everybody else at Cheyenne Mountain, knew the SL-13's were capable of carrying nuclear warheads. But, like everyone else on both sides, at least in the lower echelons, he had grown indifferent about them. Living for so long in the tangled shadows cast by thousands of Titans and Minutemen and SL-3s and SL-9s, the checkered shade seldom caught his eye and, more seldom still, cost him a wink of sleep.

"Lieutenant, tell Colonel Meyers I'll be along. I want him to open comm lines to the Pentagon and the White House."

"Yes, sir."

Kowalski saluted again, turned crisply, conscious of how meaningless his pirouette would be if the blip on the war-room screen meant what it could mean. Sprinting back through the barren maze of concrete and steel, his steps echoed hollowly from the high ceiling. The lights were dim, broken here and there by the garish red of an emergency lamp.

Kowalski had been at Cheyenne Mountain for three separate tours. The excitement of being part of the most secure installation in North America had long since worn off. By the end of his first tour, it had become one more military post, harder than most to get in or out of but otherwise not much different.

Now, with the SL-13 arcing rapidly toward North America, he thought he might be one of the privileged few. Cheyenne Mountain was widely rumored to be more vulnerable than advertised, especially to a direct hit, but hell, if he went, there would be damn few other around to laugh about it.

Kowalski careened through a doorway, its heavy steel doors bracketed by armed guards. The sentries knew something was up and eyed him hopefully as he ran past. A scrap of news, even a rumor, would be welcome. It had to be the worst duty in the whole installation, standing there, back to the uproar, wondering what the hell was going on.

Colonel Charles D. Meyers, the duty officer, was pacing nervously as Kowalski bounded down into the snake pit. The very heart of the central control room had been so named early on, before its hundreds of miles of cable had been permanently installed and hidden from view. The engineers who had charge of its construction, frustrated by the thousands of links and tangled coils, had named it, and it stuck.

Even General Collins used it, much to the dismay of ranking civilians in the Defense Department. It smacked too much of the sinister and the uncontrollable. Four times in two years, memos had gone out enjoining use of the nickname. Too little, too late.

Charlie Meyers, hands clasped behind him, eyed the delicate trace of the SL-13 on the colorfully illuminated world map high on the south wall. He stopped in mid-stride, resting one hand on the casing of a huge Cray supercomputer, one of several tied into his network. The fastest computers in the world, even they were taxed by the intricacy of tracking thousands of variables and calculating nearly infinite possibilities.

The logic tree was one of the less helpful tools of modern philosophy, in Meyers's judgment. In more placid moments he couldn't help but wonder what Wittgenstein might make of a logic forest like the one grown up around the concept of defending North American airspace. And if one of those trees fell in the bewildering forest, would anyone be alive to care whether it made a sound?

"General Collins is right behind me, Colonel," Kowalski said, panting. "He wants open comm lines to the White House and the Pentagon, sir."

"Very good, Lieutenant."

Meyers had anticipated the order. The lines were already open. Washington, he knew, would already be abuzz with rumors. You couldn't do anything the least bit out of the ordinary anymore, without some asshole picking up the phone to dial Jack Anderson or Bob Woodward.

The Crays, their display lights flashing in a bewildering carnival of color, felt warm to his touch. It wasn't a real problem. The controlled temperature would handle the extra heat, if the circuits didn't overload. The problem was making sense of what was going on in the time allowed. A worst-case scenario made that less than fifteen minutes.

Meyers glanced at his watch, then looked up as the heavy steel doors clanged shut on the gallery above him. General Collins was already halfway down the metal stairs.

"Colonel, what's going on?"

"I don't know, sir. The Soviets have thrown something up from Plesetsk. It's an SL-13, according to all incoming data, but it's not on a normal trajectory."

"Estimated target?"

"Looks like Seattle, General."

"Looks like?"

"Yes, sir, looks like. It changed course a couple of minutes into flight. Until then it looked like a satellite dump. Then things went haywire. The trajectory is skewed, unstable as all hell. The best I can do right now is a probability curve."

"Seattle, you say?"

"Yes, sir, but that's just a guess. Seattle is toward the southern edge of the possible target area, but it's the only major U.S. city in the running."

"Colonel, that's hardly an appropriate phrase. We are not talking about competition for the next Olympic site."

"Yes, sir. Sorry, sir."

"Have you reached the White House?"

"Yes, sir. The open line is in the backup control room."

Collins glanced up at the electronic map. The soft green line had grown still longer since he'd entered the main control room.

"I'll be on the phone, Colonel. Keep me posted. And if there's any change, any at all, I want to know immediately."

"Yes, sir."

• • •

The lead elk sensed something. It stopped, extending itself, stretching like an aerobics instructor. Stock-still, ears twitching like spastic radar, it listened. Overhead, the whistling debris began to rain down. Still out of sight, it whistled and hummed.

The elk looked up. With a bellow it began to run. Behind it, the herd began to ripple, a brown sea in the ragged white-and-green expanse. Moving south, to winter grazing land, it surged, nose to haunch, as far as the eye could see. In the gathering frenzy, animal after animal took up the bellowing call.

It was mid-morning, the sun nearly as high in the sky as it would get. The clumps of snow, left from the first pre-winter storm, stood out like small mounds of white fire against the gray-green tundra.

Trailing small plumes of smoke and flame, the shattered wreckage of the SL-13 fanned out and down. Some, still burning, sputtered in the melt water from the permafrost. Some, larger than most, landed with perceptible impact. And the largest, still relatively intact, slammed home with audible thunder, smoking wires and twitching cables reaching out like thick, desperate nerves searching for some comfort.

The metallic hail pattered and hissed over a twenty-mile strip, the smallest, lightest pieces landing first, most susceptible to the drag of the atmosphere, while the largest roared on, torn between gravity and momentum. And when the last, and largest, piece of wreckage had fallen, the elk were gone, their frightened lowing an eerie echo in the pale Arctic light.

And around the world, in Plesetsk and Colorado, Africa and Australia, Washington and Moscow, anxious men huddled around small, flat screens. They had no more idea than the elk what had gone wrong, but unlike the frightened animals, they knew something had.

Something had gone unpredictably, desperately wrong.

Major Schevardnadze paced nervously, hands restlessly folded behind his back. The last delicate tendrils of contact still glowed softly on the giant monitor. The control room was silent; even the dull buzz of whispered conversation stilled, less by the ordered silence than by stunned amazement. Through the glass he could see General Gribanov, his stony, normally pale face a writhing pink mask. His jaw, as he listened, bunched noticeably, even at this distance. And when he spoke, his lips moved stiffly, as if he had difficulty forming the words he needed. Once, an angry sweep of his arm knocked coffee flying, its dark brown spew splashing the glass window and trickling down in chocolate-colored rivulets. Schevardnadze watched the coffee pool on the ledge, then cascade over the edge and down out of sight. Gribanov's adjutant, normally so efficient, stared at the coffee in rigid silence.

Soon, he knew, there would be questions. What kind of questions he couldn't guess. The payload was a secret. The questions, as so often in the secret-ridden society that was the Soviet Union, would seek to elicit information while yielding none to the uninitiated.

Well, he had seen it before, though never from the perspective of the questioned. He would tell them what he could. The best thing to do was forget about trying to discover the source of their concern and pay attention to the questions, looking for the disguised trapdoors and hidden panels in their logic. One misstep and he would get to see the top of the globe . . . if he was lucky. Still, Siberia wasn't the end of the world. And there was always a chance that his answers would be the right ones. Who really knew who was to blame when no one was quite sure what the crime might be?

Gribanov seemed to be winding down. His voice started to regain some of its force, a dull mumble now through the glass. His movements became less like those of an automaton. Perhaps, Schevardnadze thought, things weren't as bad as they seemed.

They had lost rockets before—often. More often than anyone, even those in the rocket command, would have guessed. It, like everything else in the Soviet Union, was rigidly compartmentalized; everything was on a need-to-know basis. And the one thing no one seemed to need to know was how often things got screwed up.

At first it made him smile to read accounts of Western disasters. How smugly they were reported. Small balloons blown by the hot air of State news reports into magnificent zeppelins of American incompetence. But lately he had grown weary of the myopic analysis. The long view, the only truly acceptable view, was that the planet was too small for the bloated egos of the superpowers and their tunnel-visioned custodians. He felt like a naïve romantic whenever he drifted into such thinking, but in his heart he knew it was undeniably true, no matter how romantic it seemed.

General Gribanov wheeled suddenly, handing the telephone to his startled adjutant. He banged through the heavy door into the main control room, gesturing to Schevardnadze as he whisked by. Without breaking stride the general swept out of the control room and into the long underground tunnel connecting the nerve center of the base to the underground residential quarters.

Schevardnadze had to sprint to keep up with his commanding officer. Their footsteps echoed hollowly on the concrete walls of the tunnel.

"General, where are we going?" Schevardnadze asked, struggling to keep up.

"Not we, Major, you. You are going to find the wreckage of that rocket, and you are going to bring it back."

"But, General, that's impossible. It could take weeks to find it."

"We don't have weeks, Major. We have five days. No more."

"It will take longer than that to get permission from the Canadians."

"Only if we ask, Major, only if we ask."

CHAPTER 3

Luke Simpson looked out over the desert landscape.

The hard-edged sun was sliding down behind the mountains, its blood-red disk muted by the purple stripe at the edge of the world. As soothing as he usually found sunset, tonight it seemed strangely oppressive.

He was expecting company. It was business, and that didn't make it any more pleasant. He'd had his fill of stuffed shirts. His own man now, after pushing a broom for their ilk far too long, he still got uptight when he had to sit down face-to-face.

Their incompetence, and their unwillingness to admit it, had driven him from their midst. Their inability to do anything about it made him richer every day. He should have been happy they couldn't get it together, but it just made him mad. Too many people needlessly suffered because of it.

Stuffed shirts were bad enough, but when they wore care labels stamped "Made in Washington, D.C.," his gorge rose at the mere anticipation of a meeting.

Add the word *undersecretary* to a man's name and you could almost tell what he'd look like. The carefully clipped hair, the understated cologne, even the goddamn jewelry, just bold enough to call attention to itself without seeming brazen, were hallmarks of the earnest, not quite so young men still kidding themselves that they were on the fast track.

Undersecretaries of Defense were no different. They might talk out of the sides of their mouths, like third-rate impressionists having a go at the Duke, but they were still undersecretaries. None of them seemed to realize exactly what it was they were under, or what the smell was. Maybe that accounted for the cologne.

Luke stared through the tinted glass, counting saguaros to pass the time. Rank on rank, the cactus marched across the empty flatness. As far as the eye could see, they stood, all shapes and sizes.

Sentries, guardians of an all-too-precious solitude was how Luke thought of the plants, their existence testimony to the persistence of life in the face of incalculable odds. He preferred their company to people—most people, anyway—and knew it made him a bit of an eccentric, at least to those who had never spent a reflective hour in their company.

He disliked, too, the manufactured urgency of the Washington temperament. The frenzy seemed so unnecessary, and would have been, if only the peculiar animals who lived there would tend to business in due course, instead of waiting for a problem to become a crisis.

Luke glanced at his watch, mesmerized by the steady sweep of the second hand. In ten minutes, given the federal compulsion to punctuality, Mr. Undersecretary Ralph Tompkins would walk through the door. He would be brisk and no-nonsense in his approach, just a trifle impatient—the only way he knew to hide his embarrassment for being there.

Luke stared into the low distance. A dark blue bubble, like an embolism, slid along the narrow vein of asphalt. In a few seconds it was identifiable: a late-model Buick, governmentally sedate and chromeless. The big car stopped as if the driver were lost. Luke smiled. How lost can you be when the place you want is the only man-made thing in sight? Or was that a foolish question?

The car jumped forward again, so suddenly Luke imagined

he could hear the squeal of its tires on the scorching road. It passed out of sight to the right, beyond the window frame. It would, Luke knew, now be slowing to turn in through the stone gatepost that marked the edge of his compound. The first speed bump would catch the driver by surprise, scraping his muffler on the graveled tar of the broad driveway.

Luke turned in his swivel chair, flicking his wrist to turn on the TV monitor mounted over the door to his office. On its large screen, in muted color, Luke watched the Buick bounce to a halt near the main entrance. Two men got out of the front seat, identically attired in dull gray suits and mirrored sunglasses. The only difference between them was four inches and fifty pounds. The driver, the larger of the two, and apparently also the younger, stepped around the hood and opened the rear door on the passenger side.

Luke watched, a half-smile on his lips, as the ideal bureaucrat slid out of the car, his briefcase clutched tightly in one pale fist. The man was a couple of years younger than Luke had anticipated but otherwise conformed to expectations.

Ralph Tompkins had come to ask for Luke's help. In a few minutes Luke would know why. A few moments later Tompkins would know whether or not his trip had been wasted.

The Undersecretary disappeared from view. A moment later voices, obscured by footsteps on the hard wood of the corridor, announced his presence in the building. Leaning back in the swivel chair, Luke turned his back to the doorway and waited.

Carmela knocked timidly before entering. "A Mr. Tompkins to see you, Mr. Simpson."

Without turning Luke said, "Show him in, Carmela. Thank you."

When he finally turned to face the doorway, Tompkins, point man for a flying wedge of three, stood spread-eagled just inside the door. He held his briefcase in front of his knees, gripped tightly by the handle with both hands.

"Simpson, I'm Ralph Tompkins." The Undersecretary cleared his throat before continuing. "You were expecting me, I think?"

Luke nodded. Gesturing to a chair with his left hand, he stared at the two shaded men accompanying Tompkins. Luke didn't need to see their eyes to know they were flat and humorless. Some nondescript color like hazel or gray. Their faces were expressionless; they looked like the Secret Service in Hollywood movies, and for good reason. It was one of the few things Hollywood got right.

Tompkins sat nervously on the edge of the chair, balancing his weight carefully, ready to stand or lean back, depending on the next cue. Luke let him dangle.

The man was stylishly thin, his pasty complexion and pale hair appropriate for a nocturnal or cave-dwelling animal. Luke put his weight at a hundred and fifty pounds, give or take a couple, and his height at the national average. Pale blue eyes, red-rimmed as if their owner had been crying recently, darted curiously around the room. When it was obvious Luke intended to let him take the lead, he leaned forward.

"This is . . . very nice. Not at all what I expected."

"Oh, and what did you expect? Ninja robots in the halls?"

"Well, of course not. It's just . . . your reputation, you know. It led me to certain assumptions."

"That's the trouble with reputations. And with assumptions."

"Yes, well, I suppose so."

"You didn't come here to discuss my reputation, though," Luke said.

"No, I didn't. Actually I—that is, we—are in a bit of a bind. We wondered whether you would be available—for an appropriate fee, of course—to lend a hand."

"That depends."

"On what?"

"Lots of things. Like, who is this 'we' you speak of?"

"Why, I thought you knew. The Department of Defense, of course."

"I know you are from the Defense Department. I don't know who you represent." Luke smiled without amusement. "You'll have to forgive me, Mr. Tompkins, but I've been around the block a few times. I know enough about Washington to know that very little is what it seems. Just because you draw a paycheck from Defense doesn't mean that's where your loyalties are, or where you take your orders from.''

"That's absurd, Mr. Simpson. I've never heard of such nonsense.''

"You're either younger than you look, or the Ivy League has relaxed its standards for matriculation.''

Luke got to his feet. Tompkins sank down into his chair, a puzzled look on his face. Luke crossed the wide expanse of the office to stand with his back to the floor-to-ceiling window. Framed by the desert, hands folded behind his back, he waited for Tompkins to turn in his direction.

The Undersecretary glanced uncertainly at the mirrored eyes of his companions. They remained impassive. Solid and utilitarian, like bookends from Dunhill.

"Why don't you get right to the heart of the matter, Mr. Tompkins. I can ask questions if I need to. But do us both a favor. Save the horse manure for your garden in Georgetown. Just tell me what I need to know to make up my mind.''

Tompkins nodded as if he understood. Choosing his words carefully, he got off to a slow start. "There has been an unusual occurrence. A . . . an event that—''

"Just tell me what happened.''

"The Soviet Union has launched an experimental rocket. It caught us by surprise. It . . . we don't know what to make of it.''

"How does that concern you or me? They launch more experiments in a month than we do in five years.''

"Of course. But this one is more unusual than most.''

"How do you know?''

"We have—unofficially, of course—been sharing information about all launches for several years now, ever since the NORAD computers went haywire a couple of times in the seventies. Neither side wanted to take the chance that a surprise launch might be misinterpreted. You can see the wisdom in that, I guess.'' Tompkins paused to scrutinize Luke's face, perhaps looking for confirmation. When Luke said nothing, he continued.

"They didn't tell us about this one. That alone makes it unusual. But there's something else."

"What?"

"Before I can tell you, I'll need your signature on these documents." Tompkins clicked the latch on his briefcase and reached inside. He withdrew three sheets of letter-size stationery and held them out for Luke.

Curious, Luke stepped toward the seated man and took the papers. Stepping back to the window, he turned his back to read the form. It was, in triplicate, a confidentiality agreement. By his signature, Luke would agree to reveal nothing discussed with Tompkins and that violation of the confidentiality agreed to would subject him to forfeiture of any and all fees he might otherwise be entitled to receive, not to mention fine and a rather lengthy imprisonment, at governmental discretion.

"This agreement plays fast and loose with my civil rights, doesn't it, Mr. Tompkins?"

"Not really. It is simply a formality. We want you to understand how seriously we hold this information."

"Mr. Tompkins, bureaucrats—you'll pardon the expression—hold all paper sacred. Truth and responsibility somewhat less so, I'm sorry to say."

"Do I take it you refuse to sign?"

"I didn't say that. I just want you to know the spirit in which I sign." Luke snatched a pen from his shirt pocket and scribbled his signature three times on the dotted line. Handing the executed documents back to Tompkins, he smiled sardonically. "You may continue, Mr. Undersecretary."

Tompkins ignored the sarcasm. He tucked the signed agreements into his case and snapped it shut. He nodded to the larger bookend, then paused until the latter had shut the office door.

"I don't mind telling you, Mr. Simpson, that I consider the engagement of your services undesirable. Be that as it may, I have my orders."

"Then you're a good German, Ralph."

"The rocket, an SL-13 as far as we can determine, malfunctioned. It was lost some minutes after launch."

"Lost? How can it be lost? Everybody and their brother monitors anything larger than a softball that gets off the ground."

"I don't mean vanished, exactly. I mean catastrophically lost. It veered off-course and exploded. The debris was much harder to track. We have only a vague idea where it landed, someplace in northwestern Canada, and no idea at all what it was."

"So what am I supposed to do?"

"Find it. Quickly."

"Why me?"

"Because we are interested in expedient recovery."

"By expedient, I take it you mean extra-legal?"

"Not exactly."

"But approximately? After all, there are simpler ways to go about it. You could call the Mounties, for example. They always get their man. Some space junk ought to be a piece of cake for Sergeant Preston of the Yukon."

"This is not a matter to be taken lightly, Mr. Simpson."

"I can see that. And just what do you expect the Russians to do while I'm off skiing in Jack London territory?"

"We don't know. Since the launch itself was extraordinary, there is some reason to believe they may attempt to recover it themselves. Without recourse to diplomatic channels."

"So it's a sled race, eh?"

"Look, dammit, Simpson. I'm here on a matter of the utmost importance to national security. I'm getting damned tired of your snide remarks. Either you're interested or you're not. Now, which is it?"

"If you're so damned tired of my snide remarks, why don't you quit coming off like every other tight-assed bureaucrat in that sinkhole of ineptitude we call the nation's capital and tell me what the hell is going on. You waltz in here like a fucking prima donna, giving me your goddamn papers to sign like I was some high-school recruit. That isn't how I do business, and it sure as hell isn't how the other side does business. Now, if *you* are interested in *my* services, you'll cut the shit and tell me everything I need to know."

Luke stared at Tompkins for a long minute. The Undersecretary of Defense returned the stare. Luke could almost hear the wheels turning.

Tompkins stood abruptly and walked to the door. Opening it, he gestured to the hallway. "Wait outside," he said, showing the Hardy Boys the door.

"Now you're talking." Luke smiled.

CHAPTER 4

High on the ridge, Colonel Arkady Borlov scanned the valley beneath him with binoculars. The third day of the operation, it was the worst weather day so far. Morale was bad enough among the troops without compounding the problem. He wondered whether all the trouble was worth the so-far elusive reward. Who really needed Afghanistan?

Like his men, he had been getting short of temper in recent weeks. Six months was too long a tour, but anything less than that was impractical. The men, mostly draftees, cared little about the war and less about their officers. Watching his own back was something that did not come easily to him.

Borlov had read almost everything written by American officers on the conduct of the war in Vietnam. The parallels were too striking for any but the most determined ostrich to ignore. The *mujahideen* were fighting out of the same fierce nationalism and desire for self-determination. That in itself should have been sufficient warning. But the *mujahideen* were also as masterful as the NFL at exploiting the home-field advantage.

Now in its eighth year, the invasion of Afghanistan showed no signs of winding down. It had taken the United States little longer than that to pull out of a bad situation. How long, he wondered, would the Kremlin ostriches ignore that fact?

Across the valley, on the far wall, which, unlike the gentle slope before him, rose nearly a thousand feet straight up, he could see no evidence of the enemy. But then, that was to be expected. Confronted by overwhelming superiority in weaponry and unlimited firepower, only a fool would show his face. And the *mujahideen* were no fools. They wouldn't have held out this long if they had been.

Borlov turned crisply, like a good soldier should, and climbed carefully back to the ridge line, his knee-length boots slipping in the loose scree that littered the slope. On top again, he stamped his feet to rid the boots of dust. He examined them carefully, noticing the dust-filled creases at the instep. He bent to wipe them with a glove, then looked at the sky, still down on one knee.

The familiar whomp of the choppers echoed up from the valley floor. Air support, at last. Far below and to the east, Borlov could just make out five shiny specks—Mi-28 helicopters gliding effortlessly over the broken rock and ankle-deep dust.

He grabbed the field glasses again, zeroing in on the first copter. An awesome machine. Sleek as a cruising shark, its stubby wings loaded down with rocket pods and machine cannon, the chopper swooped back and forth, trying to cover as much ground as it could in a single pass.

The *mujahideen* were down there somewhere, probably near the base of the steep rock face. The choppers, strung out in a sinuous, undulating line, curled along the mountain wall like a sidewinder, gliding to within a few yards of the wall, then dodging back out.

The lead copter suddenly climbed straight up. Its pilot must have seen something. Borlov heard the straining engine, wound tight, whine like a manic buzz saw as the chopper rose. A puff of smoke on the valley floor, paying out a tin filament of grayish-white, pursued it. The hand-held missile slipped past, narrowly missing its target, just as the *whump* of its launch rolled up the slope.

Obviously the *mujahideen* were packing some of the U.S.

Stinger missiles smuggled in from Pakistan by the overland route. It was hard work for so little hardware, but the kill ratio was disconcertingly high. In the last three months alone, more than fifty helicopters had been lost. Borlov didn't envy their squadron commanders trying to explain such a high casualty rate.

Following the lead chopper, the other four rose vertically, leveling off at five hundred feet, high enough to give the pilots some maneuvering room. A second plume of smoke rose, almost from the same spot, and this time the hidden rocketeer had a better aim.

The fifth chopper in the line, still climbing, vanished in an orange ball, then an oily cloud. Bright bits of metal spun out of the roiling mass of smoke, spiraling away and down like a handful of cheap diamonds.

The four remaining choppers backed off, then spun into a fan-shaped curve, a semicircle around the launch point. Hanging back, they zeroed in. Borlov watched the rocket pods swivel noiselessly, imagining the shrill whine of their servos as they homed in.

As if controlled by a single nerve, all four choppers cut loose at once. Thick, whitish smoke obscured the pods, then was torn to rags by the rotor wash.

The thunder rolled up from below, lagging seconds behind the fire blossoming at the base of the cliff. Thick black smoke rose in concentrated columns, climbing on the currents of super-heated air. A second salvo, a little more ragged than the first, roared home. This time the bursts of flame were muted by the coiling smoke. Again the thunder climbed up the slope, like a wave of sound beaching itself in exhaustion.

Behind him, Borlov heard the half-hearted cheers of his troops. Most of them couldn't care less which side got the better of the engagement, as long they could get back to the barracks in one piece and hang on until they were rotated out. Borlov didn't blame them. If there was anything worse than war, it was deliberately fighting an unwinnable war for no discernible reason.

Borlov knew that's what his men thought they were doing. And not just this latest bunch. Almost from the beginning the troops had sensed the foolishness. This was Borlov's third tour, and only now was he beginning to see what his men had understood immediately: There was no reason to die for Afghanistan.

The choppers had emptied their rocket pods. Now they began to swarm like angry hornets, their 30-mm cannons rattling in a steady racket.

It was time to move.

Borlov hopped into his jeep and gave the signal. The column, largely infantry in armored personnel carriers mounted with light artillery and a few four-wheel drive vehicles supporting heavy machine guns, began to wind down the rutted crease that passed for a road. The frequent switchbacks tripled the descent time, but there was no other way. The slope was too steep and the rocky debris too loose for a more direct approach.

Borlov pushed his driver to speed up but knew it was pointless. By the time the column reached the valley floor, the *mujahideen*, if they survived the aerial onslaught, would long since have vanished into the crags and crannies, slithering away like reptiles at home in the terrain.

More than anything else, it was the futility that got to Borlov. It wound him tight, like a brittle spring. He tossed away most nights, his teeth grinding until his jaw ached. The tension and the helplessness were breaking him to pieces.

Three more weeks—that's all he had to manage. As short as that time seemed, there were times—too many lately—when he wasn't sure he'd make it. He wasn't worried about getting killed in action. That would be a relief of sorts. What he feared most was losing control of himself, breaking down like a battered child, crying himself out of a career and into a rest home.

If it weren't for his father-in-law, he wouldn't even be here. But the family name had to be upheld. His wife's father, General Zukovsky, was commander in chief of the eastern front. It wouldn't do for Arkady Borlov to shirk his responsibilities. Like in the West, it was the politicians' sons who got the favors and the soft duty. The army brats had to show how tough they were, eating nails for breakfast and horseshoes for lunch.

Still, it was only three weeks.

The column had wound through the last switchback now. The choppers were still hovering but had ceased firing. Borlov didn't know whether to be happy or not. If the pilots were satisfied the enemy had been routed, they would have radioed in and beat it back to the base. Obviously something was still moving on the ground.

Borlov pulled to the side, standing in the jeep and waving the column on. When the last APC had rumbled past, his driver fell in behind it. The thick dust Borlov had grown to hate was rather sparse in the heavy, humid air. He removed his hat to pass one hand through his thinning hair, brushing a few unruly strands away from his eyes. The cold wind was beginning to whip up.

The sun, almost illusory all morning, had finally vanished altogether behind the thick cloud cover. When the wall was less than a kilometer away, Borlov felt the first flakes of snow. Cold on his cheeks, they melted almost immediately. A swirling veil of snow descended suddenly, and the rock wall disappeared.

Quickly Borlov radioed to the lead APC. The armor was no protection, not against a determined man with a magnetic charge on his belt. Blindness made them equals. The wind began to howl, ripping the snow like tattered cloth across Borlov's field of vision. The column ground to a halt. His jeep pulled off the road and raced ahead, groaning against the slippery scree. Already Borlov noticed the snow beginning to stick to the cold rock and sifting down to mingle with the dust.

The valley was a natural collector, heavy snow dumped by the enforced climb over the mountain falling eagerly and collecting rapidly. By the time Borlov reached the head of the column, the vehicles were already white everywhere but over the engines, whose heat was enough to melt the snow for the time being. The swirling snow mixed with fuel-laden exhaust, painting the entire column a ghostly grayish-white.

As his jeep skidded to a halt Borlov noticed a dark mass,

like a shadow, moving haltingly toward the lead APC. Turning his head, he watched out of the corner of his eye.

A sudden sprint and the shadow assumed more solidity. It leapt for the APC.

Borlov tried to yank his Makarov automatic from its unwieldy holster. The flap got in his way, and he had to try three times before getting the heavy handgun free.

The shadow skidded across the top of the APC and ducked down behind the machine-gun turret. A disklike shadow appeared over the turret. The hatch was being opened. Borlov aimed, straining to see his target. The hatch banged down and Borlov fired. The shadow fell backward. Borlov leapt from the jeep. Landing recklessly, he slipped on the snow-covered scree.

Getting to his feet, he began to run. With a wrenching squeal, the APC opened like a can of peas. The blast rumbled and vanished into the swirling snow. Ruptured metal and black smoke took its place.

The impact knocked Borlov to his knees. He knew what was coming. Covering his head and neck, he burrowed sidewise in the snowy rock. The fuel tanks went, almost in tandem. Something tugged at his left leg.

Borlov spun around to a seated position. He felt a hand on his shoulder. "Colonel Borlov, are you all right?"

Stunned, he looked up into the puzzled face of his driver. The kid seemed surprised at all the noise. Black smoke mingled with the driving snow, momentarily obscuring his face. When it reappeared, Borlov had regained control of himself.

His leg ached. He looked down, almost detached, at the sliver of steel protruding from the trouser leg. The pants were already soaked with blood. He reached down, grabbed the sliver tightly between his fingers, and yanked. A sharp pain shot through his left calf. The wound was painful but not serious.

"Let's get out of here, Lieutenant," Borlov said, struggling to his feet. He waved off the driver's arm and limped back to the jeep.

Grabbing the radio mike, he ordered the column to seal all

hatches and surrender its position. The clang of hatches being secured was drowned out by another explosion. A second APC, farther back in the column, vanished in a cloud of smoke.

Borlov climbed into the jeep and screamed into the mike. The heavy armor began grinding its treads, maneuvering for a one-eighty. Borlov stood in the jeep, peering into the thickening snow. It was already too late to prevent casualties. He could only hope it would be possible to salvage the rest of the column.

The slippery switchbacks were no longer possible. Borlov ordered a retreat through the wide end of the vee-shaped valley. Last in line, his jeep struggling against the slushy muck churned up by the APC tracks, Borlov stared over his shoulder and wondered what the hell he was doing there.

The twenty-five kilometers back to Chahardeh seemed to take an eternity. It had been negotiated with no further losses, and Borlov was sitting, pantless, on an infirmary table, congratulating himself on minimizing the damage. As the medical officer placed heavy tape over the gauze wrapping, Captain Lavrenty Mikhailov poked his head in.

"Colonel Borlov? General Gorky wants to see you as soon as you're through here." He snapped a crisp salute, then smiled. "Don't worry, Colonel, it's good news. You've got a special assignment. You're getting the hell out of here. Three weeks early."

Borlov smiled thinly. "One day too late for eight good men," he thought.

CHAPTER 5

The two Antonov An-124 Condor transports sat idly, their powerful turboprop engines rumbling in the cold. The rear decks were open, gaping like the mouths of panicky whales, gulping the cold in huge swallows. Night had fallen quickly.

Gregor Schevardnadze stood silently, watching the thin clouds of exhaust spiral up and away into nothing. The frigid air was dry, insatiably dry, swallowing what little moisture survived the twenty-below temperature.

This was going to be something new for him. A different kind of operation from anything he had ever known. Leaning against the corrugated hangar wall, he realized he should have been excited. He had wanted a change. Well, here it was, and he was scared. It wasn't what he had in mind. Somehow, deep in his gut, he knew this was a misadventure, something he'd never tell his grandchildren, even if he lived long enough to see them born. And how unlikely that all seemed to him now.

In thirty minutes he would be leaving everything he had known totally and completely behind. He could look out a window and watch if all fall away, like the dry, transparent skin of a shedding snake. And, like the snake, he lacked the tools to know what would replace it. Novelty used to appeal to him. But not anymore.

Behind him, the clatter of green troops, like schoolboys preparing for a picnic, echoed in the bowels of the huge metal building. They had been trained, of course. They were better prepared for this kind of operation than he would ever be. But preparation was no substitute for experience, for that gut instinct that came with years of army life.

Borlov, that pompous ass, had drunk himself silly. "In celebration of the new assignment," he said. The buffoon had downed nearly two liters of vodka the previous night. That was not conduct calculated to inspire confidence. Colorful, maybe, but not inspirational.

The army was different now, so changed from what it had been. Maybe his father had been right; maybe the old ways *were* the best ways.

But he had never listened. How tired he had grown of hearing about the glory days, how the bitter Ukrainian winter killed more Red soldiers than all of Hitler's armies. Those were the days, all right.

The clatter behind him grew louder, more organized. As the science attaché, he had little command responsibility, and less influence. He might as well have been an instrument, all wires and transistors, as a man. A machine's opinion would probably carry more weight.

Borlov was busy across the hangar, arguing with someone out of his view. There was something about Borlov that disturbed him. The man seemed to have some edge to him, a burr under his saddle. Explosive irritation prompted by nothing, unpredictable rage, even tantrums, were part of Borlov's command arsenal. In the eighteen hours he had known Colonel Arkady Borlov he had grown to detest him.

The hangar was under the tightest security Schevardnadze had ever seen. Even tighter than that surrounding the launch. GRU types were everywhere, watching everything. KGB was watching GRU and vice versa. In two hours Schevardnadze would finally get his orders. Maybe then he would know what all the secrecy was about.

He ground another butt under his heel, blew a long cloud

of breath out into the wind, and turned back to the work at hand. He was responsible for the electronic equipment, some of it so far unidentified, purpose unknown, being loaded into the cargo bay of one of the two huge Antonov air freighters. The unmarked crates were ferried into the plane on wheeled wooden pallets, three forklifts taking turns with the equipment.

The cargo crates were strapped shut and tied in place, then a small army of coveralled men labored to attach the heavy cargo chutes on which they would be launched into thin air. The two Antonovs were far too heavy to risk a landing. The equipment, whatever it was, would be at the mercy of a not-so-soft airdrop.

Not knowing what it was, Schevardnadze tried to forget about the substantial question of whether or not it would work after uncrating. He felt like a fool, watching the mysterious gear disappear into the yawning jaws of the plane.

Borlov spotted him, waved a gloved hand, and gestured to him. Schevardnadze debated whether to ignore the wave, pretending he hadn't seen it. Borlov was a time bomb waiting to blow, and Schevardnadze wondered why he seemed to be the only one who heard the ticking.

Unwilling to risk offending the quixotic colonel, he walked slowly across the floor to the hangar, threading his way among the antlike columns of workers. He felt like a condemned man asked to tea by his hangman. It was a vague, simmering discomfort, one he couldn't shake.

Borlov started to move toward him, as if impatient to begin their conversation. He was still several meters away when his voice boomed above the racket in the hangar. "Major Schevardnadze, is your equipment loaded?"

"Not yet, Colonel."

"Well, hurry up. We are already behind schedule."

"I wasn't aware of that, Colonel. I haven't been advised of any schedule."

"Well, I have. And we are late."

"What time are we scheduled for takeoff?"

"As soon as possible, Major."

"Then I guess I *am* late."

"It won't do to take this mission less than seriously,

Major. It is of the utmost importance to the motherland. Not to mention our respective careers, eh?'' Borlov winked, as if trying to apologize for his aggressiveness.

Schevardnadze eyed him warily. He wanted to stay on the man's good side but so far had difficulty locating it. He sighed heavily.

"Something wrong, Major?"

"No, not really, Colonel. I'm just nervous, I guess. I'm not used to this sort of duty."

"You technical people don't really have duty. You have science, isn't that true, Major? There is nothing particularly military about the kind of work you do."

"Maybe not, Colonel, but we are accustomed to military discipline and accept the additional responsibility it requires of us."

"I hope so. This is going to be one for the history books, Major. You are privileged to be a part of it."

"I'd like to appreciate it in that light, Colonel. But I don't have any idea what's going on. All I know is that something went wrong and we are going to clean up the mess. Hardly calculated to inspire awe or an awareness of history, don't you agree?"

"Major, consider yourself fortunate. I have just returned from Afghanistan. *That* is military duty. And if you screw up there, you screw up for good. This will be infinitely more interesting, and far less dangerous. Nothing but polar bears and Eskimos to worry about."

"I wouldn't be so sure of that, Colonel."

"Why not?"

"You don't think the Americans are going to sit back and watch, do you? They must have tracked the rocket. They must know what has happened to it."

"Ah, but they have no idea how significant it is, do they?"

"Colonel, even I don't have any idea. In fact, I'd be willing to bet you a bottle of vodka that the Americans know more about it than either of us."

Borlov held a finger to his lips. "Major, the monkeys have ears. And GRU is not noted for its appreciation of irony. You'd do well to bear that in mind. They are likely to be as

interested in the listener as the speaker. I, for one, have no
intention of trying to explain your sarcastic wit to one of
them. I shouldn't think you'd enjoy the prospect, either.''

"I'll keep that in mind, Colonel." Schevardnadze saluted
and turned sharply. Walking back to oversee the loading of
the last few crates, he passed the second plane. He stopped in
his tracks when he saw the cargo being hustled aboard. The
cargo bay was full of motorized sleds, several mounted with
.50-caliber machine guns. It looked more like an invasion of
Finland was being planned than a scientific recovery mission.

Crates of ammunition and containers of fuel were lined
against the outer fuselage of the huge freighter. He shook his
head in disbelief. Before he could recover, he felt a hand on
his shoulder. Turning, he realized Borlov had been watching
him.

"Well, what do you think, Major?"

"About what, Colonel?"

"Impressive, isn't it? One thing I learned in Afghanistan is
to appreciate the opportunity to get whatever you need. This
was my chance to write a blank check. Everything I wanted, I
got."

"Are we going to take Ottawa, Colonel?"

"Hardly."

"We won't need all those weapons, surely."

"Maybe not, Major, but once we're in, we're in to stay.
We can hardly expect to be resupplied at the drop of a hat.
And eighty men need a lot to keep them going in the wilder-
ness. I want to be ready for anything."

"It looks like you're more than ready. It looks like you're
eager."

"I'm not sure there's a difference, Major."

Schevardnadze walked off, shaking his head. The suspicion
that Borlov was coming unglued kept gnawing at him. The
man seemed to be spoiling for a fight. If he lost his head,
none of them would be safe.

Schevardnadze suppressed a shudder as the last crates rolled
up into the planes. His intuition was working overtime. Borlov
was bad news. But what could he do about it? He was second
in command of the mission but didn't even know who to go

to. And if he did, he wasn't sure he could explain what was bothering him.

Borlov was a combat veteran, while Schevardnadze hadn't fired a weapon in three years, and then only on a qualifying target range. Maybe Borlov was the perfect choice. He couldn't even address that question without knowing what they were expected to accomplish.

Schevardnadze checked his watch. In less than an hour they would be airborne. It would be too late to do anything then. Practically speaking, it was already far too late.

He'd have to grin and bear it. The toughest part was knowing that the men were Borlov's men, not his. Although he was nominally second in command, the men would look past him to Captain Chertok and on down the chain of command. As far as they were concerned, Schevardnadze might as well be a civilian. He was excess baggage, and he knew it.

CHAPTER 6

Luke stared at the telephone. For a moment he picked the receiver up and cradled it on his shoulder. Reaching forward to push the buttons, he stopped. Getting to his feet, he placed the receiver back on the phone. A moment later he was in the garage. He had to talk to Ben Sanchez. But face-to-face was the best way to do it.

There was no question that he was going to take the assignment Tompkins had proposed. But, like most complex things, the acceptance preceded understanding. Talking to Ben would clear his head. Ben's logic, unconventional by academic standards, was rooted in a deep understanding of how the world worked, the kind of understanding that only distance can give.

The desert stretched ahead all the way to the horizon. Low hills marked the Mexican border, but that was far to the south. A hundred miles of the Sonora desert stood between Luke and Mexico.

Luke covered the distance without being aware of it. Ben lived in a trailer with his wife and daughters. Times were rough enough for Indians in Arizona, but rougher still for one who wanted to be a cop. It was what Ben did, and he did it well, despite the fact that ends seldom met. Moonlighting for Luke was the only thing that kept him afloat.

The two men hadn't seen each other in a while, but time seemed to mean nothing to their relationship. Luke couldn't count the number of times they'd let months go by without talking. The bond was stronger than time and distance, even stronger than that which ties brother to brother and father to son.

When he reached the trailer, nestled in a small stand of cottonwoods near the only decent water for miles around, Luke knew instinctively that Ben wasn't there. He parked, anyway, and hopped down from the high perch of his 4×4. He crossed the neat but decidedly Spartan front yard and knocked on the screen door. The inner door was open, but Luke preferred to wait outside. After a couple of minutes he knocked again, this time not expecting an answer. Neither Ben nor his family was at home.

Luke walked around to the back, his boots crunching on the yellow gravel most Arizonans used as the base of their cactus gardens. Unconventional in so many respects, Ben was aggressively conformist in this one. The small chollas and prickly pears, thickly fleshed against the arid climate but well taken care of, seemed even more alien against the metal walls of the trailer then they did in the wild.

On the back door a note was tacked with a small fishhook. "Out back." That was all it said. Luke smiled at the joke. Looking over his shoulder, he stared into the desert stretching away until it met the sky, so blue and cloudless that it hurt to look at it.

And somewhere out there he would find Ben.

If Deadly Force were to have a chance on this assignment, they would need someone attuned to the limitless expanse, the mountain wilderness. Luke had more than enough to drawn on if all he needed were warm bodies and plenty of guts. But this time he needed more than that, much more. He needed a man who could smell the peril, who could hear the truth just below the wild wind.

Luke watched the parallel ruts of his 4×4 in the rearview mirrors for a moment. They stretched off toward the horizon, dwindling to a single strand before vanishing altogether. The sparse, dark green ground cover told him there had been a recent rain. He knew enough about the desert to guess from the dust that it had been a few days ago. But only an Apache like Ben could tell him how much rain had fallen and, within an hour or two, precisely how long ago. That kind of intimate understanding of nature made Ben indispensable. Not that he had any particular experience of the Arctic. But he had the rhythms of the earth in his blood; his heart beat its complex patterns in time to them.

Ben knew.

It was that simple.

The fine soil, a thin, claylike dust, was broken less and less often now by vegetation. Ben's trailer had disappeared from the rearview. Here and there a saguaro jutted up into the cloudless sky; clumps of teddy bear and chain cholla and prickly pear cast their spiny shadows. Luke hadn't seen so much as a lizard for the last half hour. But Ben was out here. Luke knew that. And he was convinced he could find him.

Dead ahead, a low butte suddenly broke over the horizon. It wouldn't be more than five miles away. Luke gunned the engine, swerving occasionally as he drove. He was certain Ben was at the butte, probably camping in its shade.

The threadlike cloud thrown up by the 4×4 smeared itself across the sky behind him, ripped by a hot wind.

The butte was drawing closer. It couldn't have been more than seventy-five or eighty feet high. How it had come to be in the middle of such a flat wasteland, miles from the nearest kin, was for the geologists to consider. Luke was simply grateful for its existence. As he approached within a half mile of the butte, Luke stopped the Bronco. He scanned the base of the butte, looking for some evidence that his hunch was on the money.

A bright gray smear caught his eye off to the left, and he grabbed his binoculars. He zeroed in on the smear, and Ben's battered gray Blazer with its big-foot tires leapt into sharp focus. The Apache was here, all right. Now all he had to do was find him. No, that was wrong. All he had to do was sit and wait for Ben to find him. That was how it usually worked. And that, after all, was why he had come to the desert in the first place.

Luke shut off the engine, parking his Bronco alongside the Blazer. He jumped down again, his feet kicking up small clouds from the bone-dry soil. He reached into the rear of the Bronco and jerked a pair of powerful Zeiss binoculars over the bucket seat. The glasses banged against the steering wheel, and Luke cursed his carelessness.

Walking a few steps away from the cars, Luke popped the lens covers off and turned the glasses on the precipitous rock wall of the butte. Close up in the precision glasses, the wall was even more forbidding than when viewed at long range. But such formations were full of secrets. Ben, most likely, was somewhere on top, having worked his way up the rocky face by using hand- and footholds no one else would suspect.

He worked back again, this time moving the glasses more cautiously, stopping at every shadow. Still no Ben.

Luke let the glasses fall. He'd have to wait for Ben to come back on his own. He turned, still toying with the glasses dangling around his neck, trying to get the lens covers back in place with one hand.

"Pardon me, but those are my feet you're stepping on."

Luke came to a halt, slamming into the rock-hard body of a man he hadn't known was there. For a second it startled him. Then, recognizing the boots, he cursed good-naturedly.

"Ben, you son of a bitch. You spooked me."

"I meant to. You long-knives had better learn to make less noise, if you want to make a go of it out here."

"Long-knives? I thought we were 'white eyes'?"

"That was last week."

"How do you like snow?"

Ben scanned the sky, craning his neck, as if to get a better look at it. "Be a while before we have any."

"Not here, wise guy."

"You going up to Aspen, you crazy, rich guy, you? Sure, I like skiing. When do we leave?"

"Tonight. And it's not Aspen."

"Tell me about it." Ben walked over to his Blazer, threw a canteen into the open window, then sat on the sand beside one of its massive tires.

Luke, already in breach of the confidentiality agreement

he'd signed for Tompkins, sketched the bold outlines of the assignment. Ben interrupted from time to time, asking for more detail or clarification of an obscure point. When he had finished his summary, Luke looked expectantly at the Apache.

"What do you think?"

"I think a man has got to be crazy to accept an assignment like that."

"I know, but what do you think?"

"It could be done. It all depends on who we have to beat, and how many."

"That's all guesswork at this point."

"When isn't it?" Ben said.

Luke knew Ben was thinking of another time, and a place just as hot but infinitely greener than the Sonora would ever be. The Indian stood up and walked off a few yards, his back to Luke and the cars. He looked up at the massive stone formation, like a man trying to read a message written in letters too large to read at close range.

Ben bent suddenly, snatched at the sand, and lifted his hand cautiously. He still hadn't spoken. If Luke didn't know the man as well as he did, he might have assumed the Apache had forgotten all about their previous conversation.

"You know," Ben said, "people are afraid of all sorts of things, for all sorts of reasons. Sometimes they're right to be afraid." His voice was almost a whisper, as if he were speaking in a church vestibule. He extended his hand toward Luke. The thing he'd snatched from the hot sand sat perfectly still in the center of his hand. "But then they're afraid of things like this too."

The banded tarantula cocked its head and seemed to be listening to the man who held its life in the palm of his hand. "Things aren't always what they seem," Ben continued. "You have to look past the surface, see how things really are. Then you can decide what risks are worth taking and what ones you ought to pass up. This thing won't really hurt me. And if I'm lucky, somebody'll give me ten bucks for it."

"What are you saying?" Luke asked.

"I could use the money."

CHAPTER 7

The hatch opened, sending a howling echo the length of the fuselage. Schevardnadze inched forward; his hand danced in a spastic clutch on the ripcord. He looked at the thin nylon tether and wondered what the hell he was doing there.

The wind grabbed at his jumpsuit and whistled, like a sarcastic critic evaluating his clothing. Behind him, eighty men huddled, babbling in stage whispers. Like him, they were already tethered to the steel cable that would spare them the exertion of ripping the cord themselves. Unlike him, they were all veterans of airdrops. Schevardnadze hadn't jumped since basic, where airborne tactics had been only a footnote to his more esoteric education in the ways of the military.

Borlov, he knew, was watching him closely. And scattered among the others were the usual complement of GRU types and KGB clones. That was to be expected.

What surprised him was the presence of two (so far unidentified) *spetznazi*. Why they were present was speculative only, and it chilled him to the bone. The avant-garde assassins of the Soviet steamroller, they could only mean trouble. Rare as genuine Fabergé eggs, they were widely discussed and seldom seen. More often than not, it was the ruined shells of their victims that testified they had passed by. He wanted to think about it, to ponder the implications of their presence. But now he was too frightened to be sure of his name, let alone exercise a tenuous hold on logic.

Three men stood between him and the door. Then two. When the third had gone, the wind smacked him hard, like a sharp hook from a quick welterweight. He hadn't been hit that hard since his Olympic boxing aspirations were knocked out of him in the final elimination round before the '76 games. He looked down at the blue-black void, concentrating on the tips of his jump boots. The bulky suit seemed to smother him. A slap on the back and he let go, eyes closed, feeling the wind rip him back along the underside of the plane.

Eyes still closed, Schevardnadze felt the jerk of the chute, heard it flutter, then snap open. He was sure there would be a battalion of Canadians to welcome him below. Briefed on the flight plan, he had been assured that what their low altitude wouldn't hide, their radar jamming would. But Schevardnadze indulged the uninitiated's healthy skepticism of things he cared too little about to try to understand.

The drop was mercifully short but too long by half. Slitting his lids, he looked up past his parachute to stare at the storm of mushrooming shrouds above him. Even at this distance he could hear the sharp crack of chute after chute popping open. Looking down, still through slitted eyes, he could see the gray mass of the Earth whitening as it rushed toward him. The screech in his ears grew louder.

Schevardnadze tried to remember all the rules his instructor had screamed at him. Like a long-forgotten litany, they leapt back into life—but they failed to cushion the shock as his feet made contact.

His knees were full of molten lead; his hips threatened to come undone. He yanked the shroud lines and rolled. The half-empty chute dragged him several meters before he got it under control.

He struggled to his feet, not too embarrassed to watch the others landing around him, most so nonchalant they might have been out for a Sunday stroll in Gorky Park. When the fascination wore off, he struggled out of his harness. The last three or four parachutes were less than a hundred meters above him. All around him, men clanked at their buckles and tugged at their leather straps. He strained his eyes in the dark, wondering where Borlov was.

The wind was bitter cold, but the ground was still relatively free of snow. The stars were sharp above him, glittering like bits of ice in the clear night sky. When the last chute had collapsed, he bent to gather his own, yanking on the lines until the shroud, billowing and pulsing like a live thing, was at his feet.

As he bent to gather it into a compact mass, he heard his name called from the darkness. The voice belonged to Colonel Borlov. "Major Schevardnadze? You there? Anybody seen the major, or did he hitch a ride home already?"

The others, cued as much by the colonel's tone as by the words themselves, laughed dutifully. Schevardnadze, anxious to put a stop to Borlov's manipulation, shouted into the dark, "Did the colonel send a tape recording to keep us amused? Or did he come himself?"

The others laughed again, this time in genuine amusement. A voice behind Schevardnadze whispered, "Take it easy, Major. He's one mean son of a bitch. Take my advice. Don't cross him."

Schevardnadze wheeled to see who had spoken, but the dark was cluttered with shadowy figures, none of whom betrayed the words of warning.

Shrugging like a dog ridding himself of cold water, the major wrapped the slippery fabric in its lines and squeezed it tightly into a ball. It wasn't neat, but it would serve the purpose. The chute would never be used again, anyway.

A moment later Borlov materialized out of the darkness. He strode toward Schevardnadze as if he had known all along where the major had been. Planting himself alongside the technical adviser, he stared at the sky. "Look sharp, Major, there's a lot of freight on the way down. It would be a pity if something were to land on you, eh?"

"No danger of that, Colonel. Not with you along to look out for me."

"You'd better hope so, Major. Things can get out of control very quickly, out in the field. But that's something a desk jockey like you wouldn't know much about, is it?"

"Colonel, if there's something on your mind, it might be best for everyone, especially the men, if we were to settle it here and now."

"There's nothing on my mind, Major, nothing at all. And don't talk to me about the men. That's something you know nothing at all about. I am a field commander. I've lived with these men, and with men like them, for twenty years. I'll look out for them."

"I'm sure you will, Colonel. Maybe we should just make sure there's nothing between us. To be on the safe side."

Borlov ignored the suggestion, as if he hadn't heard it. "Major, I'll want your suggested procedure for the search as soon as the equipment lands. Make sure you've got something intelligent to say."

Schevardnadze saluted, the gesture almost absentminded in its execution. "Yes, sir, Colonel."

Borlov strode off, his feet crunching on the permafrost and vestigial vegetation. Small depressions were filled with a dusty snow, reminders that the weather could turn at any moment. Schevardnadze shook his head and turned his attention to the sky, where the thunder of the lead Antonov, coming in for its second pass, had begun to fill the night.

The freight, some of it dangling from clustered chutes, began to drift earthward. The pallets still trapped in place, the drop could be made from close in with considerable accuracy, more like a bombing run than an airborne assault.

The first crates had already landed. The men stood huddled together, anxiously watching the sky to make certain nothing strayed off course and disappeared in the darkness. And they were just as anxious that they not be brushed by an errant crate.

The second cargo plane roared past, its cargo bay spewing freight on billowing chutes like a manic dandelion. In fifteen minutes the sky was empty of everything but the howling wind.

The men labored over the crates with snips and crowbars,

freeing up the load in efficient teams. Borlov wandered from team to team, his hands clasped behind his back. Schevardnadze supervised the uncrating of several pieces of equipment, pitching in with a crowbar and stripping the slats with an efficiency born of anxiety. It helped him to lose himself in the sweaty work.

Glancing at the sky, he was disturbed to see a thick overcast rolling in from the northwest. Its leading edge seemed to boil like a breaking whitecap as it pushed southeastward. The front was moving like a locomotive, pushing heavy winds ahead of it. The stars disappeared behind the boiling lip of the weather. The blackness overhead was dwindling rapidly, its place assumed by the dark gray of heavy weather.

Working on the last crate, Schevardnadze felt the wetness of the first snow, the brittle flakes melting in the beaded sweat on his bare neck. He shuddered at the first touch of cold, then bent to his work with renewed energy. As each instrument was decrated, it was loaded into the rear of a half-track, itself only recently detached from its parachute sling.

The half dozen instruments were linked together, the modular cables then plugged into the main power bank of a heavy-duty portable generator. When the last instrument had been loaded and wired, Schevardnadze climbed into the half-track. By the ruddy glow of the red work lights, he clicked each power switch in turn, waiting for the intricate pattern of internal checks to blink its way through a series of LEDs.

The programmed sequence of beeps and twitters soon attracted a small crowd around the rear of the half-track. When the last instrument had run through its preliminary paces, Schevardnadze turned his attention to the centerpiece of the small mobile laboratory, an IBM System 38 minicomputer, pirated piecemeal from Western Europe. It was the heart and soul of the instrument package. Without it, nothing else was of any value.

The second most vital piece of the instrument package was a sensitive radio scanner. The SL-13, and its payload, contained several transmitters. Most were tied into the rocket's main telemetry data transmitter, but it was possible, even likely, that one or more of them would continue to function.

No longer tied to the main comm unit of the SL-13, nevertheless they might still be sending out weak signals that Schevardnadze might be able to detect. His sealed orders had given him extra details, particularly on a ROM-based signal scanner to be linked to the System 38. That had only partially explained the most mysterious component of the cargo.

The unit also contained a satellite link to enable the insertion team to communicate with a monitoring station located on the tip of Sakhalin Island, either directly or via a satellite relay.

Also included, for reasons that so far escaped him, was a radiation detector. There was nothing in the normal SL-13 that was radioactive.

That could mean that the payload was hot.

It wouldn't, or certainly shouldn't, have been a nuclear weapon. But knowing what it wasn't, didn't help him know what it was. So he was looking for something unknown. The prevailing attitude seemed to be that he'd know it when he found it. That, in itself, was unsettling. Looking for it with Borlov peering over his shoulder was less comforting still.

There was the chance, of course, that the transmission link, once established, would be used to convey information otherwise withheld. But that didn't seem likely. If it was information too sensitive to entrust to him, it was unlikely that the Kremlin would risk the possibility of an intercept. The Cosmos and Molniya satellites were marvelous devices. But like any piece of technology, they were decipherable and comprehensible. If the payload was sensitive enough to warrant the kind of security he had seen at Plesetsk, Lenin only knew what it might be.

The half-track groaned as Borlov climbed in through the rear. "Major, are you all ready?"

"In a moment, Colonel. I just have to run a couple more routine checks."

"Very well. The rest of you, clear out. The major and I will be busy for a half hour." Indicating two noncoms in the gathering, he continued, "You and you, make sure we have a secure perimeter. Thirty meters. No one comes closer. Not even yourselves. Is that understood?"

"Yes, Colonel Borlov."

The noncoms immediately assumed the officious air of underlings entrusted with great responsibility, however, transitory. They began herding the others before them, using their rifles as goads.

When they were alone, Borlov waited patiently for Schevardnadze to complete his readiness checks. The chirping of the equipment seemed to irritate the colonel. He stared at the glowing LEDs as if they were responsible, not only for the noise but also for the current situation.

"This junk is all well and good, Schevardnadze, but it won't take the place of one good soldier."

"It's not meant to, Colonel."

"For my money, we would be better off spending our rubles on better infantry weapons, newer field technology. This exotic garbage is a waste of good silicon."

"Electronics is not meant to replace the foot soldier, Colonel. It is merely supposed to help him to his job better, and maybe keep him alive longer. Laser sighting technology, for example, makes our T-72 battle tanks much more effective."

"Those tanks are a product of the propaganda mills, Major. I don't know if you've ever seen one in the field, but they are disasters. They are vulnerable to a simple helicopter thirty kilometers away. The right missile wins nine out of ten times."

"Perhaps, but the missiles themselves use much the same technology. Perhaps it is the tank itself that is worthless. Maybe time has passed it by."

"Major, you don't have any idea what it's like in the field. Don't lecture me."

"I was merely playing devil's advocate, Colonel."

"Well, don't. He has advocates enough without you. Take it from one who's been to hell and back."

CHAPTER 8

"All right, here's the story. I'll make it short and sweet."
Luke Simpson turned his back to the five men and clicked on
a monitor overhead.

Deep underground, in the Deadly Force facility, they were
anxious despite the solidity of the fortress. Luke, more than
the others, had misgivings about the undertaking. But he'd
been pointing out the clay feet of most federal agencies, or
bad-mouthing them, depending on who you listened to, for so
long that he felt it was the only reasonable attitude to have.

The monitor glowed a deep blue-black. Another click and a
map of Alaska and Northwestern Canada flickered on the
screen. "I been there," Calvin Steeples said. "Nice country.
We going fishing?"

Simpson suppressed a smile. "Not hardly, Calvin. And
you should recognize it. This map is the result of your
photo-reconnaissance work. Much digested by Dr. Cao."

"He does more than chew that damn betel shit, don't he?"
Calvin mumbled.

The display was the result of two years of work. Luke had
commissioned PR studies of virtually everyplace Deadly Force
might be required to work its lethal magic. The project was

less than half finished, but Luke had concentrated the initial efforts in the Western Hemisphere.

He had pushed Steeples and Cao, and despite frequent grousing about slave labor from Steeples and Yankee imperialism from the crusty Vietnamese, they had done yeoman work.

Ben Sanchez, as was his style, said nothing. The Apache leaned back in his chair, scrutinizing the display thoughtfully. It was territory he'd never seen. He'd always planned to go, but luck was uncertain and money short. And he wasn't delighted about the prospect of seeing it under these circumstances. He knew more than the others, except Luke, about the project. It was their biggest opportunity to beat the feds at their own game. There was no way in hell Luke could afford to pass on it.

"Now, here is the area we're interested in." Luke clicked another button, a soft green circle appeared on the screen. Its focus was Ammerman Mountain. Its radius was too large to suit anyone in the room. By half. Ammerman, at the northern limit of the North American forest, was inhospitable terrain at the best of times. The forest, north of the Bluefish River, was barely worthy of the name. The tundra north of it, all the way to the Beaufort Sea, was even worse. To the east was the tangled Mackenzie River delta, a wilderness of permafrost and sinkholes big enough to swallow the Taj Mahal and still have room for the Louvre. To the west, nothing but the Alaskan wasteland. All of it was north of the Arctic Circle.

"Luke, that's a tall order," Cao said.

Luke nodded.

"It's a given, Tran. We can't narrow it down any further without some additional intelligence."

"You don't find much of that in D.C.," Calvin volunteered. The others laughed uncomfortably. They preferred not to be reminded.

"The haystack is approximately ten thousand square miles. And I have no idea what the needle looks like. It's there, we're sure of that. But that's about all we're sure of. We don't even know what kind of shape it'll be in."

"What's the big deal?" Steeples asked. "Why can't we

wait for spring? Hell, salvaging junk ain't exactly my favorite thing, at least not in the snow.''

"Because in the spring it won't be there.''

"Why not?''

Luke looked at Sanchez, who nodded slightly. The Apache had been briefed as fully as the sketchy information permitted. Luke had wanted to wait before spilling the whole story to the others. He thought better of it now. He took a deep breath.

"Because we may not be the only ones looking for it. Think of it as sort of the granddaddy of all scavenger hunts, if you will.''

"Who else is playing?'' Steeples asked.

"For sure?''

"Hell, no! Best guess is what I want.''

"Ivan.''

"All right, Luke, my man, you better paint the big picture. And spare none of the gory details.''

Quickly Simpson ran through the events of the last twenty-four hours, insofar as they were known. He spared no reasonable conjecture or educated guess. When he had finished, he paused to let it sink in. His audience of five took a collective breath. It was the only sound in the room.

Finally Ben spoke up. "When do we leave?''

"As soon as we get all the equipment together.'' Luke checked his watch. "That should be in three hours.''

Calvin raised his hand slowly, little more than shoulder-high, as if he weren't sure he wanted the floor.

"Calvin? You want to say something?''

"I was just wondering about something. I know Ben and the inscrutable Oriental here, but I don't recognize the others. How about an introduction?''

"Sure. I was just getting to that. You sort of disrupted my agenda.''

Steeples laughed easily. "I seem to make a habit of that, don't I?''

Luke smiled. "Why don't you two step up here a second while I introduce you?'' he asked, gesturing to the raised platform on which he stood. The two newcomers rose stiffly, obviously ill at ease with such formality.

Either of the two men easily would have been the biggest man in the room if it hadn't been for the presence of the other.

If linebackers were bookends, Luke had a matched set. The two-hundred-fifty-pound range was a good guess for either. At six four and six five, their height offered a means of discrimination only to the discerning eye.

"This is Mr. McCarthy," Luke said, introducing the man nearest him, and the taller of the two. Turning to the other man, he continued, "And this is Mr. McCarthy."

"Twins?" Steeples sounded as if he disbelieved it.

"Fraternal." The McCarthys smiled.

"You got first names?" Calvin asked.

The larger man responded. "I'm Patrick, and this is Padraic."

"Shit, that's the same goddamn name."

The shorter man smiled. "If you prefer, you can call him Patty and me Paddy."

"Thanks for the help," Steeples said, sitting down again and shaking his head. "I better work it out for myself."

"Look, we have a bit more to get through here. Why don't we get on with it. I want to be in the air as soon as possible. You guys can get acquainted on the flight." He turned back to the soft green glow of the monitor.

All eyes turned to the map again. The circle still dominated the display, but it seemed to be immeasurably larger. Steeples wondered whether it was growing, like a live thing. Then he pushed the thought out of his head. Their problem was big enough without such nonsense cluttering his mind.

Luke completed his briefing in crisp, concise language, conscious of the clock on the wall behind his audience. When he was finished, the men clustered around him, each babbling his own special set of concerns. Luke didn't blame them. The problem was formidable, the odds against success astronomical. And worst of all, a condition had been imposed on him, something he usually resisted. He was going to have an observer along. Allegedly from the State Department, but Luke new better.

The CIA was going to be watching him.

Malcolm Conroy was waiting impatiently in Luke's office. When he heard the door open, he looked up anxiously. An intelligence analyst, he was not used to being away from the womblike insularity of Langley. It was his first field assignment. Luke hadn't cared for him on their first meeting but recognized that the young man was nervous. When things settled down, maybe he'd be palatable.

Luke, himself, had spent some time in the same position, but he chafed under the routinized boredom. He knew, and the agency knew, that he was cut out for operations work. Why he had ended up processing news clippings and sifting through raw data still puzzled him, even more than it had galled him at the time. After a few months of feeling like a trained chimpanzee, he had left. To say there were no hard feelings would be less than honest.

Conroy got to his feet. Luke noticed the young man bouncing nervously from foot to foot, his trousers dancing in place with nervous energy. "How'd it go?" he asked.

"It went. That's all I can tell you."

"Can't or won't?"

"Look, Conroy. I'm not happy you're here. You know that already, I should think. But I agreed to tolerate it, provided there is no interference. But I'm warning you: You get in my hair and I shave my head. You understand?"

Conroy took a step back. He stared at the tall, rugged man before him like an anthropologist attempting to categorize a new species of *Homo sapiens*. He didn't seem happy with his discovery.

"Look, I have a job to do here. I have my orders. How can I carry them out if you don't cooperate?"

"I'll cooperate. But I'll decide when and how much. I'm on a short fuse, and so are you. But my fuse is shorter. I have a job to do too. No pin-striped yuppie from Yale is going to get in my way."

"It's Dartmouth."

"What?"

"Dartmouth. I went to Dartmouth."

"Yeah. Boola, boola. Ivy's ivy, Conroy. Just stay in your cage and everything'll be all right."

"I can have you removed from this assignment."

"Oh, yeah? Who'll you get to take over? I have this job because I'm the only one who can get it done quickly. You want to find somebody else, do it. And tell your bosses I'll bill them for expenses incurred so far. Fair enough?"

"You're serious, aren't you? You really would walk out on this."

"I never joke with Ivy Leaguers, Conroy. They're out of my class. Recognize your limits. That's the best way to make a go of it in this world. The *only* way. And now that I've pointed yours out, please get ready. We're leaving in an hour."

Luke turned to leave the office.

"Simpson, can I use your telephone?"

Luke indicated the instrument on the corner of his desk. "Help yourself. Leave a quarter in the cup."

By the time Conroy realized what he meant, Luke was gone. The door hissed softly closed, and Malcolm Conroy was left alone, to analyze what he'd learned so far.

Luke took the elevator down to the hangar. Buried under the Superstition Mountains, it could accommodate the old B-36, and would—if Luke could get his hands on one. The old beauty, long in the tooth, and long since relegated to aviation history by the B-52, had been Luke's favorite leviathan as a kid. Old loyalties died hard, and Luke, while appreciative of the B-52 and hopeful that the B-1B was more than a pipe dream with a high price tag, still missed the tingle of his first exposure to high-performance aircraft.

The Saberjet and the B-47 were relics, the F-100 almost as hoary, but they still claimed pride of place in his heart.

The collection he had so carefully built over the recent past, when his unexpected windfall had made it possible, even easy, to afford, had opened old wounds and rekindled nearly dead embers. Luke wanted to keep it all alive, the old and new.

The giant C-5 Galaxy cargo plane was going to get them where they needed to go. The flight-readiness crew looked like Hummel figurines on maneuvers, as they dashed around on the concrete floor far below him. The glass elevator gave him a clear view of the gargantuan craft.

Its two-hundred-and-twenty-foot plus wingspan, seemed more appropriate to some prehistoric era, when monstrous brutes walked on the Earth and the air belonged to dinosaurs. It surely was too large for anything but such gargantuan company.

Jake O'Bannion, Luke's crusty, rotund alter ego, had skipped the briefing in favor of overseeing the cargo assembly and loading. A phone message had asked Luke to meet Jake in the armory. On a lower level, beneath the concrete pad of the hangar, it harbored nearly every conceivable useful weapon, in quantity where possible.

Jake, a former New York cop more than passingly acquainted with the technology of death, was the official armorer and unofficial second in command of Deadly Force. His big heart pined for the old days on the front lines, but his bigger gut was just one obstacle to that reality.

As the elevator passed through the hangar floor Luke got a good look at the underbelly of the huge Galaxy. Its camie paint job made it look like an obscenely bloated vegetable of a kind previously uncataloged.

Luke waited for the elevator to glide to a halt, then pushed the exit button impatiently. Stepping into the long, dimly lit corridor, he sprinted to the armory. Jake was pacing nervously when he entered.

"My God, boy, what took you so long? That Harvard lad gumming up the works?"

"Dartmouth, Jake."

"Whatever."

"You wanted to see me?"

'Yeah, boyo. You don't give a fella much to go on when you make a shopping list. I did the best I could, but I need to know whether you might be wanting a little extra."

"What've you got so far?"

Jake reeled of enough small arms to make a Contra leader

green with envy. "I also got them snowmobiles, like you said. They're already in the plane. Twelve of 'em, and two half-tracks for equipment and supplies. But I got to tell you, Luke. You're traveling light. Too light, I'm afraid."

"Jake, we've been through this. We have to be maneuverable. Once we get inside the search area, I want to move fast. I can't do it by air, because the Canadians haven't been informed. They probably have their own search team, if they have the intelligence data—but we're not sure and we can't ask."

"So you're goin' through with this, eh?"

"Yup."

"I'll hold the fort."

"You always do, Jake."

"Yeah. And I never like it."

CHAPTER 9

Borlov was satisfied. Splitting the team into three smaller, more manageable units, he felt he had a handle on things. Each unit had been given a sweep sector. Their data would be fed back to Schevardnadze's central monitoring facility. The new snow was already knee-deep. It was time to see just how well the tactical logic had been thought out. The units formed up and moved out.

The landing zone, until further notice, would function as the resupply base. Schevardnadze would be in command, but Borlov, accompanying the primary search team, would retain ultimate authority. A half-track and five two-man motorized sleds made up each column. The half-track, in addition to men and equipment, carried additional fuel for the sleds and for itself.

It was still snowing as the first team pulled out. Schevardnadze stood in the rear of the equipment truck, cold air rippling the fur of his arctic whites. He felt mixed relief and anxiety with Borlov gone. As the last of the half-tracks disappeared into the swirling snow, a crackle blistered through it.

Schevardnadze turned slowly, walking toward the central

comm unit. He depressed the send button reluctantly. "Ermine One, come in," he said.

"Major," the reply rasped, "it took you too long to respond. We're not playing chess out here. I want you on the controls at all times. Understood?"

"Understood, Colonel Borlov."

"You hear anything from the other units, patch me through at once."

"Yes, sir."

"And Major, by the way . . . what is the range of this radio equipment?"

"Approximately forty kilometers, Colonel."

"So little?"

"It was considered discreet, Colonel. The Americans have rather sophisticated monitoring equipment. We didn't want to risk a stray signal alerting them we were here."

"They probably already know, Major."

"Possibly. But valor is not the only way to fight a war, Colonel. If they don't know, the longer we keep our presence a secret, the greater our chances of succeeding."

"Save the speeches for your fellow technocrats, Comrade. Ermine One out."

The interior of the half-track glowed with a galaxy of red and green LEDs. The soft hum of equipment, broken occasionally by atmospheric electrical discharges, was all but drowned out by the pulsing generator outside.

Schevardnadze thanked his stars for the cloud cover. The American intelligence satellites would have a much tougher time picking up anything unusual through the dense overcast. He almost hoped the weather would remain so the rest of the time they were here but knew it would be a mixed blessing, at best.

The next three days were critical, not only for recovery, but also perhaps for Schevardnadze's career.

The search teams each carried radio detectors, looking for some vestigial signals. Stored in magnetic form, they could be sent in random bursts to disguise their programmatic nature. Schevardnadze would run the raw data through the minicomputer, looking for patterns. If anything suggestive turned up, he could plug into the Molniya satellite network, staggering his signal to the geostationary web of Cosmos units. Traffic to and from the welter of satellites was so heavy, they'd have a window of opportunity. The traffic was routinely monitored like every other kind of electronic transmission, but codes and careful transmission should still preserve their head start.

The mysterious black box, almost buried under the more familiar equipment, still puzzled Schevardnadze. He knew what it was. He just didn't know why in hell he needed it.

Something about the payload of the SL-13 was a hell of a lot more secret than anyone had let on.

The rigidly compartmentalized bureaucracy at Plesetsk mirrored that of the rest of Soviet society. Even so, rumors were rife. Everybody knew everything, or claimed to, and listened to every third rumor with bulging eyes and eager ears. Normally, that is. This launch was different. All anybody was willing to say was that it was secret. Top secret.

Now, five thousand miles away, in the middle of nowhere, Gregor Schevardnadze found himself sitting alone with a box, fifty centimeters on a side, that could answer all the questions that counted.

And he didn't want to know.

Arkady Borlov sat back in the passenger seat of the two-man sled. Removing his sealskin mittens, he pulled the drawstring on his collar, snuggling the hood tightly around his face. Smeared with protective jelly, he barely felt the sting of the wind-driven snow. Swirls of cold needles swarmed around him, rattling on his goggles like BBs, their brittle, almost metallic rhythm hostage to the inconsistent wind.

Schevardnadze was a problem. Unfortunately, however, he was a necessary one. Until they managed to find what they were looking for, that is. He had been more fully briefed than Schevardnadze. It was only fitting that a man of his superior military background have all the tools necessary for such a mission. It was too bad he had to be saddled with such a nervous nelly. But that wouldn't last. As soon as they got their hands on the shattered grail somewhere in the wilderness around them, the major was excess baggage. A minor disposal problem, he would be little trouble for the *spetznazi*.

The little fool didn't even realize he was going to be left behind, food for wolves and polar bears.

It pained Borlov not at all to think about such things. He had seen enough death and gore in Afghanistan, watched young men hold their own lives in bloody hands, seen the light go out of their eyes, jaws go slack. It would be nice to be able to win one, for a change. This was his ticket out. The bloody oblivion of Kabul would be a bad dream after this.

Borlov fingered his Kalashnikov with a stiff serenity. He was enjoying the feel of the weapon, knowing that the likelihood of using it was nonexistent. The frozen wasteland around him could have been on the moon for all the sense of life it offered. A random encounter with an Eskimo clan was remotely possible; maybe there was even a small village somewhere within their search area. But he didn't have to worry about a screaming horde descending out of the mountains, using everything from teeth to rockets. No, this was going to be easy.

Or so he thought.

Calvin Steeples filed a flight plan for Whitehorse, in the Yukon territory. Getting there was easy. The 6,500-mile range of the C-5 could get them there without a stop for refueling, but Luke wanted a stop at Seattle, for reasons he hadn't explained. From there it would get a little trickier.

The Galaxy would serve as a comm link to Phoenix, where Jake O'Bannion would handle relations with the feds. Tran Cao was going into the lab to do what he did best, find things no one else could find. The on-site team would consist of Luke, Ben, the McCarthy bookends, and two men Luke had hired sight unseen. Mercenaries out of Alaska and out of work, they had been banging around the pipeline, cutting timber, and generally watching ends not quite meet.

Steeples made the contact and vouched for them both. He'd known them during his stint as a bush pilot. Short on time, Luke took the risk. He usually made it a practice not to work with unknown quantities, but beggars can't be choosers.

The Galaxy lifted off a half hour ahead of schedule, thanks to O'Bannion's straw bossing. Watching the purple smear of the Superstitions fall away behind him, Luke came as close as he ever did to prayer. Then he disappeared into the comm center in the tail of the big bird.

Dr. Cao was already hard at work in Palo Alto. Luke raised him on the horn. "Got anything?"

"Not yet, boss. I just got started."

"Come on, Tran, time's a-wastin'."

"Luke, you demand more of your followers than the esteemed Gautama Buddha did of his."

"Maybe so, but he didn't have to worry about Ivan."

"All right, all right. I'll have something in a couple of hours. Call me when you stop in Seattle."

"I will, if you don't call me first."

Tran sighed. "Luke, that would take a miracle."

"That's what I pay you for."

"Nobody pays that well."

"What, you want a raise?"

"Raise, hell. If I deliver a miracle, I'll want more than that. I'll want respect."

"It's a deal. I can't speak for Calvin, though."

"That's all right. I'm not sure he can speak for himself."

Luke signed off, touched base with Jake, who had nothing to report, then returned to the small passenger cabin, which was separated from the cargo bay by movable partitions.

Calvin was pushing the big Lockheed's turbofans, and they whipped across Southern California like some highballing heros in a Beach Boys song. Hauling ass up the coast, they touched down at Seattle for fuel an hour ahead of the scheduled flight plan.

As soon as the landing gear screeched on the runway, Luke was back in the comm center.

Tran Cao answered immediately. "I was just going to call you, boss."

"Got something?"

"I'm not sure. Maybe."

Luke knew that Tran's caution, the only thing that had kept him alive in Vietnam, wouldn't permit a more enthusiastic endorsement of his findings.

"Talk to me."

"You got a map in front of you?"

"Is the pope Polish?"

"All right. Can you find the Bluefish River? It's in the northwest Yukon, just east of the Alaskan border."

"Got it."

"See a town called Old Crow?"

"Uh-huh. What of it?"

"I'm not sure, not yet. But I've got some pretty interesting data from NSA, and some juicy shots from the Big Bird satellite. The photos are amazing. That damn Perkin-Elmer camera shows stuff as small as a foot across. Let's hope the weather holds so we can keep using it. But I still need some more info before I hazard a guess."

"Have Jake get on it."

"I already spoke to him. The Big Bird makes its next pass in two hours. I gave them the coordinate spread. They'll see what they can do."

"Keep me posted."

"I will. Those behemoths treating you okay?"

"Who?"

"Those Irish monsters you brought along. You have enough food for them? They look like they might eat the plane, if you don't."

"Tran, you have to stop resenting everybody who's taller than you are. Five foot one leaves you too much room for resentment."

"Listen, boss. You want a miracle, you forget about my height. Just like I do yours."

Luke chuckled as he signed off. The feisty little man hated short jokes more than he hated anything in the world, including Uncle Ho, whose picture still adorned a dart board in Tran's laboratory.

CHAPTER 10

Ben Sanchez was used to the darkness, but this was different.

The desert nights he'd known were almost benign compared to the frozen hell surrounding him. Hell seemed a strange thing to call the Arctic waste sweeping infinitely away on all sides, he thought. But then, if you grew up in the dry heat of Arizona summers, what more alien place could there be?

The overcast and snow that marked their touchdown had been oppressive and intimidating. Sent out for a look around, Ben had wondered whether he'd made a mistake by agreeing to come along. But then the clouds had parted, and the sky was a revelation. The stars seemed more distant here; small, hard points of something too cold to be called fire.

The steady rumble of his motor-sled was swallowed by the night. Trees were few, and less than imposing. Ben glanced at the sky and killed his engine. Bright plumes of hazy fire spurted and danced, then winked out, only to reappear a moment later. The aurora was everything he'd heard it was. Purple and blue rags fluttered against the blackest sky he'd ever seen.

Leaving the motor-sled, Ben walked a few yards, his feet

crunching on the deep, dry snow. His neck hurt from craning back. Small clouds exploded with every breath. He continued to walk, as if entranced by the polar flares. He knew Luke and the others were waiting for him, but he had nothing to report. He had never seen anything as awe-inspiring as the spectacle above him. He might as well enjoy it while he could.

Ben dropped to his knees, taking off one thick, fur-lined mitten to grab a fistful of dry snow and crunch it in his hand. The asthmatic ping of the motor-sled engine cooling down was almost lost in the howling wind. Small swirls of snow spiraled like dust devils, then disappeared.

The roar of the wind seemed to be growing louder. It was blowing up, and a fast scud of gray slid in to cover the aurora flares. It looked like heavy weather. The moment of tranquillity was ripped now by the winds, as easily as it had tossed the snow around. In an instant Ben Sanchez was all business.

So far he'd seen nothing of importance. Noise fell dead in the snow within a few yards, as if it congealed as easily as human breath. Light was what he'd been looking for, some sign that they were not alone. Not unexpectedly, he'd come up empty.

Ben wasn't sure whether that was good or not.

Everything they'd been able to garner from intelligence sources and satellite surveillance suggested that one of the three probable Soviet units detected so far had to be within ten miles of their temporary camp. Jake, back in Arizona, was monitoring the comm lines, passing along anything new, but so far it was just embellishment on the rough outline they already had.

He might as well pack it in. No point in getting caught in a blizzard, or whatever the hell you called snow up here. Ben stood and tossed the snow back to the ground, brushing the few remaining flakes off his sleeve. He had no idea how cold it might be, but his fingers were already getting numb. He blew on the hand and flexed the fingers a few times before slipping the mitten back on.

As he turned to the motor-sled, a flicker caught his eye. He turned to face it squarely, but it had vanished. He wondered if it was one of those imaginary flashes in the dark manufactured by a light-starved eye.

Patiently Ben watched, hoping for repetition. Two minutes and nothing. Three minutes and he was sure it had been imaginary. He'd give it one more. He felt something on his cheeks, and the brittle scrape of new snow on the hood of his parka. He wanted to look at the sky but couldn't risk shifting his focus. He was counting down from ten seconds when he saw it again.

There was no mistake. It was a light—small, almost swallowed by the night and shifting snow—but it was a light.

This time it lingered in his field of vision several seconds before winking out again. He strained his ears under the wind, trying to pick up something useful. Was it on a vehicle or hand-held? He couldn't tell.

Ben ran back to the motor-sled and kicked it over. It sputtered, then caught, its low, lawnmowerlike rumble sounding louder than it was. He knew it couldn't be heard for more than twenty or thirty yards in the howling wind. Sitting on the sled's bench, he waited patiently for the light to reappear. And what, he wondered aloud, if it doesn't? He didn't want to think about that.

A few moments later the light was back. And this time it wasn't alone. The terrain ahead was relatively flat, but distance was hard to gauge. If the light was small, it could be fairly close. If it was a headlamp on a half-track, it could be a couple of miles. Now he could make out three pairs. He knew they were pairs, because they moved in concert. Probably three vehicles.

The snow was getting heavier, the flakes driving against the exposed skin of his face like hot needles. The thin jellylike glaze on his cheeks would protect him from frostbite, but the small flakes bit into him like frozen bullets.

The vehicles were moving from left to right across his line of sight, moving roughly at a forty-five-degree angle as they crossed in front of him. Ben threw the sled in gear, moving slowly, without light of his own, toward a small hill to his right. As near as he could tell, the patrol, or whatever it was, would pass fairly close to the hill. He wanted to get there first.

The motor-sled bounced over the frozen snow, its single ski rudder slapping the crust like the fin of a spastic seal. Its heavy rubber treads threw chunks of clotted snow up behind it in small arcs. As Ben moved ahead, his tracks were beginning to fill in, new and windblown snow combining to obscure all signs of his passing.

The lights seemed to pulse in the darkness. Their speed was constant, their direction as fixed as the rolling mounds of snow permitted. Two hundred yards from the hill Ben stopped, killing his engine again. He grabbed a pair of snowshoes from the rack behind him, slipped them on hurriedly, and stood up.

His Suomi submachine gun, the best the Finns could design, was draped across his back. He unslung the SMG, checked the action, and snicked off the safety. Wrapping one forearm in the gun sling, he moved toward the base of the hill.

The lights were less than a quarter of a mile away now. They seemed to be slowing down, but he couldn't wait to be sure. He wanted to be on the crest of the hill when the patrol pulled abreast of him.

The snowshoes were unwieldy, but Ben had no choice. Fissures in the snow were common here, and undetectable. Some of them were thirty or forty feet deep. Climbing out would be a matter of luck, intervention from the Almighty. It was unwise to count on the former, and Ben didn't feel all that secure in his relationship with the latter.

The slope was heavy going. Unused to the footgear, cowed by the weather, Ben struggled up the hill, wondering whether he should even be there.

Ten yards from the ridge line, he dropped to his stomach and wormed upward the rest of the way. The snow blew horizontally in the wind, whipping across the crest.

The lights had stopped. Two hundred yards away, partly obscured by snow mounds, three vehicles had come to a halt. Two of them had extinguished their lights. As he watched, the third followed suit. He could hear nothing. His instinct was to move closer, but common sense prevailed. He needed some idea of what was going on before doing anything at all.

He didn't have to wait long. A single beam of light speared out into the tumbling snow, accenting the black night all around it. Rolling on his back, Ben looked at the sky. It seemed low enough to touch. For an instant he even reached up, wondering if the clouds would fall still lower and crush him with their gray weight.

Rolling back onto his stomach, he squirmed higher on the hill, the silhouette of his white parka projecting above the snow line like a curl on a Dairy Queen. The spear of light bounced raggedly as a motor-sled eased out from behind a low mound. Even in the dim backwash of the single beam he could see the sled, its pristine whiteness unmarked. The driver, too, was a vision in arctic white. His hood was thrown back, revealing a single splash of color—a red star on his white hat, like a crimson bug on the ermine fringe of its lining.

The driver looked over his shoulder, apparently yelling something to a companion, then bounced forward, the solitary beam wavering uncertainly as the sled picked up speed. The engine must have been laboring, but Ben heard nothing but the wind.

Where the hell is he going? Ben wondered. The sled seemed to be barreling flat out toward some definite goal.

Ben wanted to get closer but couldn't, without exposing his back. He struggled with the impulse to rush forward, more than once beginning to climb over the rise and start his descent toward the encamped vehicles. It would be foolhardy, but what else could he do?

Before his patience wore through, he was rewarded. The beam reappeared, now pointed back toward the three vehicles. Ben wriggled to one side, just in time to spot the sled, now perched on a high mound, as its light was extinguished. Obviously a sentry, Ben said to no one in particular. Now he had a plan.

Slipping back down the hillside, Ben got to his feet. Keeping low, he made a wide arc.

Soon the sentry was in front of him, his unsuspecting back just a blur against the outline of the sled, fifty yards away.

Ben crawled forward slowly. Even with the wind he tried to minimize the noise. The crunch of snow would pass unnoticed. Any other sound might live just long enough to slip through one of the unpredictable lulls in the wind and carry far enough to reach the sentry or the patrol.

If he could slip up the hill, right behind the sentry, he could see everything he needed to see. The guard had chosen the best vantage point from which to see the small convoy. Ben's plan gave a whole new meaning to Russian roulette. The problem would be how to handle it if the sentry spotted him. He'd never make it if he ran.

Using a gun was out of the question. He'd have to take the guy out, but he couldn't make a sound doing it. As he slipped up the slope behind the oblivious sentry, Ben hoped it wouldn't come to that.

Even as he whispered a quiet prayer, the guard stiffened. he'd heard something. The sentry jumped up, swinging his Kalashnikov to a ready position. So much for answered prayers.

Ben slipped off one cumbersome mitten. The combat knife at his hip felt colder than usual as he bent stiff fingers around its hilt. The sentry stood beside his motor-sled. His boots sank into the down-filled ground cloth he had spread beneath him to cut down on the chill. Obviously getting ready for a lengthy stay, the man had settled in.

Ben worked to one side in excruciating silence. The sentry was twenty feet ahead of him now. He measured every step against the wind, hoping it wouldn't die on him. He timed his movements to coincide with each screeching crescendo.

Every step took an eternity. The clumsy snowshoes scraped the snow, catching in small drifts and threatening to topple over. He was too close to the man now to turn back.

The sentry stiffened, as if he'd heard something. For one eternal second the muzzle of the AK-47 swept toward him. Ben was certain he had been discovered. He steeled himself for the burst of fire. But the guard turned again, then took a couple of steps back toward the convoy.

Again Ben moved forward. Close enough to see the individual strands in the fur trim of the sentry's parka, he made his move.

He half dived and half fell, landing squarely on the sentry's back. Ben grabbed the hood of the parka and yanked backward, swinging his knife in a broad half-circle. The head reached the limit of its backward snap as the knife swept across and back.

Ben's hand felt a warm, sticky splash. Without looking, he plunged the knife into the snow, nearly to his elbow, twisting it like a drill bit as it bored into the cold purity. He lay sprawled on the dead man until the warm, sticky feeling left him, replaced first by cold, then by numbness. Only then did he dare to withdraw his hand and look at it. Blood, congealed by the cold, outlined the wrinkles in the backs of his fingers, and one broad smear still darkened his wrist.

Ben wiped the rest of the blood on his victim's virgin parka, rubbing intently, a one-armed parody of Lady Macbeth. Satisfied, he blew furiously on his fingers and slipped his mitten back on.

Time was now paramount. The sentry probably had to report in periodically. If Ben was going to get any closer, he had to do it now.

He searched the sled for a transmitter but found nothing. Rolling the corpse onto its back, he found what he was looking for. A small walkie-talkie lay on the ground cloth, sunk almost to its depth in the soft down, pressed in by the dead weight that had laid atop it. Carefully Ben pocketed the device. If the patrol tried to raise the sentry, at least Ben would know it.

Now for the hard part.

CHAPTER 11

Sliding forward on the slippery hill, Ben nearly lost his footing. Once at the bottom, he double-timed it toward the three parked vehicles. Nearing a large mound of snow, he dropped to his stomach and wiggled forward. He wanted to get a look at what they were up against.

Ben saw no movement. The vehicles were already heavily covered with snow. In a half hour they would be indistinguishable from the mounds in which they huddled. Ben worked closer and closer. He was conscious of the rasping of his arctics on the crisp snow and knew it made a noise he couldn't hear under the screech of the wind.

The vehicles were thirty yards ahead, still obscured by a large snow mound. He wondered whether he was taking a risk for nothing. No matter how many men were in the detachment, if they were inside the vehicles, he'd be able to tell Luke very little more than he already knew. Still, every little bit of knowledge was an edge. You could never tell what might make a difference.

Rolling to one side, Ben craned his neck to peer around the snow mound. It was difficult to see anything through the swirling snow. He had to get closer.

On hands and knees, Ben crawled forward. He was close enough now to see two trucks and a ski-equipped half-track, a large version of the motor-sled the sentry had been using. It looked as if it had been converted from an APC. Snow clung in ridges to invisible contours on the heavy armor plate. The vehicle looked far too heavy for use in this treacherous terrain, but the Soviets had far more experience with Arctic conditions than the U.S. He had to assume they knew what they were doing.

The trucks were conventional half-track troop transports. Less concerned with personnel amenities than Western armies, the Soviets probably expected each truck to sleep a dozen men. The APC held at least four more. That meant a minimum of twenty-eight. The small lumps arrayed to one side of the APC were a half dozen motor-sleds. Whether they represented additional men or not, he didn't know. To be safe, he'd assume they did. That made at least thirty-four.

Less one.

He couldn't hope to learn anything more without exposing himself to discovery. Right now they had the advantage. But whether surprise would compensate for the lopsided numbers, only time would tell.

He backed away quickly. When he felt he was far enough removed, he stood. Springing through the snow was no easy task. His breath came in sharp gasps. Small clouds of condensation swirled before his eyes. Making his way back up the hill, Ben heard a subdued squawk. For a moment he was puzzled. Then he remembered the walkie-talkie in his coat. Somebody was trying to raise the sentry. Good luck, fella, Ben thought. He duck-waddled on up the hill.

He had to get out quickly. And he couldn't leave any clear evidence behind. Working swiftly, Ben rolled the dead sentry onto the motor-sled. He grabbed the bloody ground cloth, rolled it into a long tube, and used it to sweep away any trace of blood on the snow, obscuring the depression in the snow as best he could.

Ben stumbled down the back of the hill, retracing his steps back to his own sled. He tugged the heavy Soviet sled behind him. Straining with the dead weight, he hauled it into position behind his own. With a length of cord he tied the two sleds together. Cranking up his engine, he swept back toward the Deadly Force base camp. He remembered the deep fissure he had seen earlier. It would make things easier if he could dump the evidence that was trailing sluggishly behind him. He hoped he could find the fissure without any trouble.

Running without lights was slowing him down. Looking for the fissure was slowing him still more. He was used to nature in less mutable forms. Dunes moved and changed shape over the course of weeks or months, but this was ridiculous.

Ready to forget it, he spotted the triangular array of snow mounds, one larger than its two companions. Fifty yards later he found what he was looking for. He approached as close as he dared, still towing his cargo. Then, stopping the sled, he untied the Soviet sled from his own and cranked up the engine. It roared immediately to life.

Ben turned the rudder, engaged the gears, and watched the sled bounce toward a gaping hole in the snow. It traveled slowly and seemed as if, like Zeno, it would never reach its destination. Then a rumble, audible even over the roaring wind, told him it didn't matter. The near edge of the fissure began to sink, then suddenly vanished. The sled disappeared in a swirl of snow, spewing out of the enlarged fissure like the smoke from hell.

In seconds the sled, along with its lifeless burden, was gone—as if it had never existed.

One down.

And thirty-three to go.

More or less.

Luke jumped like a happy kid when Ben handed him the captured walkie-talkie. While Ben filled him on his recon, Luke sat with the squawk box in his lap. A small tool kit sat on the chair beside him. Working quickly, he removed the screws holding the back cover in place.

Popping the cover, he examined the interior of the small unit. It looked like a primitive version of the standard government issue. Everything, from the printed circuit board to the molded plastic case, was closely modeled on American equipment. The chips themselves were made in the U.S.A. Three more screws and the guts were free.

Bending over in the dim light, Luke finally found what he was looking for. With a surgeon's steady hand he attached two micro alligator clips to a pair of leads, then jacked them into an oscilloscope in the comm board.

Ben finished his briefing and stood silently, watching Luke work. He admired Luke's ability to care about something so dry and fundamentally artificial as electronics. He admired it but didn't envy it. He knew things Luke would never know, things that were much more deeply human, more deeply rooted in life and its endless variations. Maybe that was what allowed them to work so well together, Ben thought.

Luke snipped a pair of leads, then depressed the transmit switch with one finger. With his free hand he twiddled a dial on the scope, waiting for the telltale wave. The placid green face of the scope seemed to stare back at Luke. Suddenly, like a small garden pond hit by a rock, it broke up in a riot of dancing light, then settled down into the familiar curves of a sine wave.

"Got it," Luke whispered, as if the unit might accidentally transmit his accomplishment. "There are a hell of a lot easier ways to do this, but you got to work with what's at hand."

"I don't see how this does us much good. We could have used this one to monitor. Besides, it's short-range stuff. We got to be close to make any use of it, no?"

"Chum, if you knew as much about electronics as you do about cactus, you'd be awesome. Fortunately for me, you don't."

"Why fortunately?"

"I got to have something to do, don't I?" Luke smiled at the Apache. "Anyhow, short-range doesn't matter. We know the frequency, so we can pick up everything with our main unit. All I have to do is patch in the megahertz value for one of our alternate frequencies, and we can listen in whenever we want. And if that isn't enough, we can tune a couple of handsets to the same frequency, so even when we're away from the truck, we can hear them if they're in range. If they're not, we don't have anything to worry about."

Ben nodded tentative appreciation, still not convinced. "So what's the next step?"

"Well, given the lopsided numbers, we can call for an air strike."

"The hell you will."

"Just joking, Ben. No, I think we have two choices. We can attempt to take them out. I don't like that option, though. There's too much we don't know yet."

"What's the other option?"

"We can let them do some of the work for us. Assume they know at least as much about the location as we do, let them do the legwork, then move in and take it away. I don't like that one, either."

"Why not?"

"Because Tran is convinced they put a pretty large unit down here. Maybe a couple of hundred men. Maybe fewer. But anyway you slice it, we're outgunned."

"So what are we going to do?"

"First thing we ought to do is listen to the bastards on the radio, try to get some sense of what we're up against. The bunch you saw might be the only one. Maybe Tran was nervous about nothing. He analyzed some data from Big Bird. It looks like two planes, both Antonovs, came through. They gummed up the PAR long enough to sneak in and out. But routine photo recon turned them up."

"Two planes?"

"Yup, Condors, and I don't have to tell you those babies haul a lot of ashes. And we got another problem. Old Crow is pretty close, inside the high-probability perimeter for recovery. Ivan wants to keep his little outing a secret. That means if he gets too close to the town, he might just do something stupid."

"Not likely, not on foreign soil."

"Afghanistan was foreign soil. So was Hungary, Czechoslovakia, and Finland a few years before you were born. . . . And this is so much easier. There aren't more than twenty people in Old Crow. You realize how easy it would be to make twenty people disappear up here? Hell, you could lose half the population of Nevada out there, and it would take months before anybody knew. Once the snow starts, there's nothing but radio contact with the outside. How long do you think it would be before anybody got worried?''

Ben said nothing. Luke was right.

Ben walked out into the snow, letting the wind whip inside his collar, feeling cleansed by the cold. He looked down at his white parka, then wiped absently at the dark, crusty smears on his sleeve.

With a final glance at the solid gray sky, marked here and there with dark patches like oil stains, hanging over his head like the floor of an infinite parking garage, Ben yanked the canvas flap of the half-track and slipped inside.

The heater was on, but he didn't feel any warmer.

"Okay, Luke. What're we going to do?"

Luke looked up from the console without answering. He stared at Ben for a long, silent moment. "You okay, Ben?"

Ben inhaled deeply, held it for what seemed like an hour, then let it out in a long, sibilant hiss. "Do I have any choice?"

"Does anyone?" Luke asked.

Ben shook his head. "No, I guess not."

Luke sat back, brooding over the information Ben had brought back. A detachment of the Red Army was sitting out there in the storm somewhere. He stared at the walkie-talkie in his hand. It seemed somehow the key, but he didn't know how to turn it.

"What do you think, Ben? How can we use this little gizmo to our advantage?"

"I thought it was advantage enough just knowing their frequency, Luke."

"Yeah, maybe. I just . . ."

"What is it? You got an idea?"

"Russian—anybody speak Russian here?"

"I don't know. Maybe one of Steeples's buddies. I'll check."

Ben disappeared, returning almost immediately with Malcolm Conroy in tow. The Company man seemed nervous, and overwhelmed by his heavy parka, like a kid wearing his father's coat.

Ben smiled broadly. "James Bond, here, speaks Russian, Luke. I told you he wasn't worthless."

Conroy looked confused. His face seemed uncertain whether to smile or to cry. When his features had compromised on petulance, Luke spoke.

"How good is your Russian, Comrade Conroy?"

Sensing an opportunity to regain what little esteem he had been accorded, he puffed himself up. "Very good. It was one of my minors at—"

"I know, I know. At Dartmouth."

"Yes."

"We'll see what kind of grade we can give you in the real world. Ben, get the rest of the guys. I want to move on this while it's still credible."

Luke and Conroy waited silently until Sanchez reappeared with the others. They crowded into Luke's half-track, the big bodies filling the place with the smell of wet clothing as the snow melted. Besides Ben, Conroy, and the McCarthy twins, their numbers had swollen to include Roland Johnson, a friend of Calvin Steeples and erstwhile bush pilot, and Mickey Martinez, a former SWAT team sidekick of Luke's from San Perplejo.

"Here's what we have to do."

CHAPTER 12

Borlov stood in the doorway, hands on hips. His face sagged under a heavy scowl. "Major, anything on Corporal Karpov yet?"

"No, Colonel. Not yet."

"I don't understand it. He went off to take up a sentry position and vanished without a trace."

"Maybe he got lost. It's so easy to lose direction in the blizzard."

"Maybe so, but his walkie-talkie should still work. Why hasn't he called in? It's been three hours. How far could he have gotten in three hours? And where is his sled?"

"Colonel, I don't know. But the answer will have to wait until Corporal Karpov returns."

"And if he doesn't?"

"Then we'll have to carry on without him."

"That's not what I mean and you know it. If he doesn't return, then obviously something happened to him. Unless we know what, we can't be certain it won't happen again. And we can't be certain our presence here is a secret."

"Colonel, we're hundreds of miles from any town or village, except Old Crow. How could anyone know?"

"Don't be naïve, Major Schevardnadze. You know, or ought to know, better than any man in this unit how easy it would be for the Americans to learn about us. You have seen satellite photographs. So have I. If you can count motorcycles from two hundred miles in space, you can count half-tracks and motor-sleds as well."

"Colonel, those are photographs taken specifically for that purpose. Random photo surveillance isn't that refined. And even if it were, the cloud cover would have protected us from any confirmation. It has not been possible to see anything since we got here. Unless someone here is sending snapshots home, how could they possibly know we're here?"

"Don't joke about such things, Schevardnadze. They are not joking matters. You forget we have company on this trip, men who live and die for such reasons."

"Colonel, surely even the GRU cannot believe that one of us is supplying information to the outside world. The very idea is ludicrous."

"To us, maybe. But they are paid to think seriously about such things. Sometimes I think they would do it for nothing, they enjoy it so much."

"Forget about it, Colonel. It isn't possible."

"And there's one more thing you should think about, Major." Borlov stepped closer to the seated major. He seemed to be deciding how exactly to say what he was thinking.

"Oh, what's that?"

"You are the only man who knows how to use all this. . . ." Borlov swept his hand in a broad arc, taking in all the twittering electronics in the vehicle. "If it occurs to me, it will occur to them. And you know how difficult they are to convince. I remember enough of my logic course to know that you cannot prove a negative, Major. At least I can't."

Borlov turned and stepped out, the truck bouncing on its tight springs at the change in weight.

Schevardnadze reached absently for the main control switch. Its shiny toggle bar seemed to elude his fingers momentarily. Finding it at last, he snapped it off. A burst of static crackled in the speaker and died. Beneath it he heard what could only be a human voice.

Quickly he snapped the power pack on. The soft hum reappeared. Schevardnadzc leaned in close to the small speaker box, perched on top of the console. The background noise snapped and cracked, its sharp, high-pitched clamor distracting. Clearing his mind of everything else, Schevardnadze concentrated on the hum. If there was anyone out there trying to make contact, they would do it again. Persistence was the only absolute.

The noise rose and fell, etching random patterns on his tympanum. Leaning closer, he strained, as if he could will a repetition of the unexplained noise. It had been human speech. He was sure of that. It was too faint to have been any of the patrols. That left Karpov. It had to be he. Schevardnadze pounded the tabletop with his fist. "Come on, dammit!" The slam echoed and died, and still he heard nothing but the trackless crackle of random noise.

But he had heard someone. He knew it. And it had to have been Karpov. The chances of some random frequency overlap were virtually nonexistent this far from human habitation. He debated whether to call Borlov back. Deciding against it, he clicked his mike open and called Karpov. His voice, he realized, was shaking. "Corporal Karpov, this is Ermine, come in."

He leaned forward again, listening. Nothing. He called again, then a third time. Each time he paused to listen. And still he heard only the crackly silence of the frozen void. Schevardnadze sighed. Once more he shut the transceiver off. He waited for a few moments, his hands in his lap.

Getting to his feet with a shrug of indifference he didn't really feel, he stepped to the rear of the half-track, opened the door, and stepped out into the cold. The wind was blowing steadily now, less fierce in its gusting but biting cold. He closed the door, then turned suddenly. He had heard something.

Cocking his head to one side, he tugged the parka hood away from his ears. The wind instantly attacked them, but he ignored it. There, again. And again. Footsteps.

"Who's there?" he called. Whoever it was began to hurry. The steady crunch, crunch of heavy boots on the new snow was barely audible under the roaring wind. Schevardnadze drew a pistol from the pocket of his parka. Uneasy with weapons, he forgot to release the safety. Holding the gun loosely in one hand, he stepped toward the noise in the darkness. The footsteps were fading rapidly now.

Schevardnadze started to run. He had gone no more than half a dozen steps when he was thrown to the ground. He landed heavily, his face slamming into the deep snow. Dimly he heard a roaring sound, then nothing.

When he came to, several men stood around him. Their bodies were starkly etched by a bright orange light, issuing from somewhere behind them. Their faces were all but obscured by the deep shadows.

One figure, standing somewhat apart from the others, stepped forward. The shadowy form knelt down and bent toward him. It was Borlov.

"Major, what happened?"

"I don't know. I was just leaving the truck and I . . ." He paused to shake his head. Everything was flickering in and out of focus; his vision blurred for a second, then snapped back. "I heard something . . . someone. I went after him and that's all I remember."

"Who was it?"

"I don't know. I never saw him. I just heard him running. He must have been right outside the truck and I . . ." Now he remembered why he had been delayed in leaving. He debated whether to tell Borlov about the strange signal, then decided against it.

"Go on, Major Schevardnadze."

The major struggled to sit up. Borlov reached into his pocket and held something out to him. "Do you recognize this?"

"It's my gun."

"Are you sure?"

"It looks like it. I remember I had taken it out. I was chasing the man when something hit me from behind." He got to his knees and pushed the gathered figures aside. As they stepped back he realized what had happened. The orange light was the glare from the blazing remains of the communications truck. One side was little more than a charred wall.

The other looked as if it had sustained less damage. Several men struggled to extinguish the flames. Their shadowy figures danced in the garish light, a vision out of Bosch.

"What happened?" Bewildered, Schevardnadze turned to Borlov.

The latter still held the pistol in his hand. He looked at it closely. "You're sure this is your gun? It's a Makarov. Is that what you were issued?"

Schevardnadze nodded. "Yes. I must have dropped it when . . . when the truck blew up."

Borlov clicked the safety on and handed it back to Schevardnadze. "A pity you didn't know how to use it." He took the offered gun and started to put it in his pocket.

"Yes, I . . . wait a minute. What did you do there, with your fingers? That click. What was it?"

"What?"

"The noise just before you handed me the gun. What made it?"

"I put the safety back on. Why?"

"Because I didn't take it off. I forgot. I always do."

"Are you sure?"

"Yes." He nodded vigorously. "I'm certain."

"Well, it's simple enough to prove. Your gun should be around here in the snow somewhere, if you dropped it."

Standing, Borlov barked at the clustered men. "Fan out there, look for a Makarov. It shouldn't be too far."

The men began to move idly in circles, scraping at the snow with the toes of their boots.

"Look sharp," Borlov snapped. "Be careful, and make sure you don't miss anything. If the major is right, we've got a traitor in our midst."

The searching men grumbled among themselves, intensifying their scraping at the snow. A couple dropped to their knees and moved carefully in circles, rubbing at lumps of snow with their mittens.

For several minutes Borlov and Schevardnadze watched silently. The colonel watched his subordinate out of the corner of his eye. Just as Schevardnadze himself was beginning to doubt his recollection, one of the kneeling men jumped to his feet. "Here it is. I've got it."

He rushed toward Borlov, his mitten wrapped around something dark. He extended his hand and uncurled the palm of the mitten. There, its trigger guard and muzzle clogged with white snow, was another Makarov 9-mm, identical to the one Borlov had handed to him.

The colonel took the offered weapon and rapped it with his free hand. The clumps of snow fell away. He brushed some stray lumps from the rear of the gun. He pushed the safety and it clicked open. Schevardnadze had been right. Borlov looked bewildered for a minute, then handed the second gun to Schevardnadze.

"If this is your gun, Major, and I don't doubt that it is, then we have a real problem."

Schevardnadze seemed not to hear him. He was staring at the burning ruins of the truck. "I'm afraid we have a bigger problem than who owns that pistol, Colonel. We have no backup for most of that equipment. If it's been destroyed, we're going to be deaf and blind."

"We'll call for another drop. We'll replace it."

"In this weather?"

Borlov looked at the sky. "What do you suggest, Major?"

"I wish I knew, Colonel. I wish to hell I knew."

CHAPTER 13

Colonel Arkady Borlov, surrounded by the leader of each squad, pored over the maps. He sketched a rough circle, the pen skipping, leaving a broken line. He slashed at the map a second time, plowing a fuzzy rut in the heavy paper.

"So, Old Crow is inside the area I want sanitized. Now."

Schevardnadze waited for the objection he fully expected to come from the squad leaders. He watched Lieutenant Genady Ekizian carefully, but even the young Armenian said nothing. When the pause lingered just a bit too long, he realized he'd have to make the objection himself.

"With all due respect, Colonel Borlov, I don't think it's a good idea."

Borlov's head snapped up. "Oh, and why is that, *Major?*" There was no mistaking the sarcastic accent on Schevardnadze's rank.

"There's no need. Not militarily, anyway. This isn't a military operation, it's a recovery mission. Why take the risk?"

"Major Schevardnadze. I will forgive your ignorance of the military necessity, something I think is obvious to the others in this room. After all, you are not really a soldier.

You are a technician, a member of a class not noted for its courage." He glared at Schevardnadze, his cheeks beginning to redden under the windburn that had already heightened their color.

Schevardnadze thought he had gotten off lightly under the circumstances, but Borlov wasn't through. "However, what I don't forgive is your mutinous disregard for military discipline. You own a uniform, and you should know at least that much about a soldier's obligations. Do I make myself clear?"

Borlov looked at each of the others in turn, ignoring Schevardnadze completely. It was apparent his delivery was intended for them, not for the major. Ekizian's jaw muscles tightened, and for a second Schevardnadze thought he was going to speak. But the moment passed. The lieutenant looked at Schevardnadze, raised one eyebrow in the briefest of shrugs, as if to say, "What can I do?" then turned away.

Borlov turned his attention to a small, dark man on the perimeter of the small circle. "For those of you who don't know him, I'd like to introduce Comrade Captain Chertok."

Schevardnadze shuddered. He knew, and suspected the others also knew, that Chertok was one of the *spetznazi* attached to their expedition. Borlov's introduction of him at this time could only mean trouble.

Master assassins and demolitions experts, the *spetznaz* agents were probably the most feared in the Soviet Army. They had no analog in any of the Western armies. More sinister than the KGB's Thirteenth Department, which was at least predictable in its paranoid insularity, they were killing machines, plain and simple.

Primarily functioning in the West as the liaison with and, as often as not, disciplinary control over, terrorist groups funded and or manipulated by the KGB, they were regarded as unworthy of discussion in polite society. Schevardnadze had even heard a member of the Central Committee wonder whether they might not have been out of control, a Frankenstein monster that ought to be destroyed at the first safe opportunity.

Looking at Chertok's flat, expressionless features and the infinite black pools that passed for eyes, Schevardnadze knew what the Committee man meant. Chertok's presence even raised the question of who was actually in charge of the expedition.

While Schevardnadze watched silently, Borlov and Chertok outlined their plan. The details about the village, and the methods with which it was to be "sanitized," clearly indicated it had been under consideration all along, either as a contingency plan or as part of the overall recovery program. In a way it didn't make any difference which it was. They were proposing an act of war.

Schevardnadze waited patiently. He tried to read the minds of the junior officers, but their impassive faces and rigid postures made it impossible. Even Ekizian, who earlier had seemed the most likely to object, betrayed nothing. At the conclusion of their presentation neither Borlov nor Chertok solicited opinions or entertained questions.

Coiling the map in both hands, Borlov looked at each man in turn. "It is regrettable, I know. But a soldier does what he must, even when he doesn't like what it is he must do." Glancing at his watch, he concluded, "We'll leave in one hour. Get your men ready."

As they filed out, Schevardnadze watched quietly. When all but Chertok and Borlov had departed, Schevardnadze spoke. "Colonel, I think this is unnecessary. I also think it's a mistake. We don't have time to go running around like this. There is little enough available to accomplish the task that brought us here in the first place."

"Major, I am in charge. I have been given complete discretion. I will decide what is necessary and what we have time for. Your equipment is a smoking ruin, thanks to someone from that village. It may be too late for you to repair the damage, but it is not too late to punish those responsible."

"Aren't you forgetting something, Colonel?"

"Not that I am aware of."

"What about the gun we found?"

"What about it?"

"It was a Russian pistol. Whoever destroyed the truck was one of us, not a villager."

Chertok started. "Is that true, Colonel Borlov?"

"Yes, but I don't see that it makes any difference."

"But it *does* make a difference, Colonel," Schevardnadze said quickly. "You are willing to risk starting a war and ignore the fact that one of your own men is guilty of sabotage, at the very least. You can't do it. Captain Chertok, tell him he can't do it."

"I have no authority to tell a superior officer anything." Chertok's tone contradicted his words. He looked expectantly at Borlov.

The colonel began to pace nervously. Finally, after several minutes of silence, he wheeled around. "All right, you may be right. But I still think we ought to send a unit to check out the village. It would be good for us to know what we might find there."

"A good idea, Colonel," Chertok said. It was obvious to Schevardnadze that he was leaving Borlov a face-saving option. "And while we do that, I think we ought to find out who is short a pistol. Let's send Ekizian's team, but we'll inspect them first and make sure they all have their sidearms."

"Major, do you have any replacements for the equipment you lost in the fire?"

"For some of it, yes, but not all. I can cannibalize some of the other equipment. Some of the instruments use modular boards. I might be able to piece something together."

"Get to it. In the meantime Captain Chertok and I will tend to other business."

Schevardnadze watched the two men move off into the darkness and the swirling snow. For some reason he couldn't quite articulate, he felt as if he had just been given a reprieve from a death sentence. He regretted it wasn't a pardon.

Climbing into the still smoldering ruins, he began to examine the wreckage. The damage wasn't as bad as he had first feared. Two units were completely ruined. They had been against the wall behind the main console and taken the full force of the explosion. The other instruments, blackened by smoke, showed no other external damage. He hoped appearances weren't as deceiving as everything else had been so far.

The blast seemed to have been directed not so much at the equipment as at the generator. Schevardnadze climbed back out of the truck. The wall between the generator, now a pile of sizzling junk, and the interior were scorched beyond recognition. The paint had been seared away, leaving broken, blistered bubbles of stiff black ash on the flame-scarred metal beneath. A large crater in the snow between the generator and the truck showed where the charge had been placed.

There wasn't much he could do until he got a new generator on line. There was no way to test the surviving instruments without power. Schevardnadze walked through the storm to the main encampment, barely visible through the swirling whiteness. He knocked on Borlov's command truck, then entered when a muffled voice barked something unintelligible.

He explained what he needed, and for once Borlov seemed too preoccupied to indulge his penchant for sarcasm. Schevardnadze left after getting assurances that a replacement generator would be installed immediately. As he walked slowly back to the battered wreck he could hear Borlov shouting orders to Ekizian.

Back in the truck, Schevardnadze began stripping the casing from the main transmitter. Working by flashlight, he unscrewed the case and wriggled the housing loose, taking care to wipe it down first to prevent any loose ash from fouling the interior.

Examining the mother board, he was relieved to see that it had sustained no damage. Some of the cables were blackened and burned through to bare wire in a couple of places. But they could easily be replaced. He replaced the casing to protect the delicate insides but left it unsecured.

Working his way along the wall, he stripped one instrument after another, only vaguely aware of the ruckus kicked up by the generator crew outside. As he explored the innards of the last instrument he heard a knock on the door. Ekizian entered in response to his summons.

"The generator is ready, Major."

"Thank you, Lieutenant. Crank it up."

"Yes, sir." Ekizian didn't move. Schevardnadze looked up at him in the dim light. Long shadows obscured the young Armenian's features.

"Is there something else, Lieutenant?"

"I . . . uh, I just wanted . . ." Ekizian stopped, his jaw slack.

"Speak up, man."

"Yes, sir. It's about before. I just . . . I didn't think it appropriate for me to argue with Colonel Borlov."

"Obviously."

"But I wanted you to know that I admire what you did. I think you were right. It was very courageous."

"You mean foolish, don't you, Lieutenant?"

"No, sir."

"Unwise, then?"

"Not in the best of all possible worlds, Major."

"But we don't live there, do we, Mr. Ekizian? In fact, such a world is not to be found in our solar system, is it?"

"Colonel Borlov is a good soldier and a good officer. I served with him in Afghanistan, Major. I learned to respect him under very difficult circumstances."

"Do you still?"

"Sir?"

"Respect him?"

"Yes, sir."

'Your loyalty is commendable, Lieutenant. But I ask you to remember one thing: Difficult circumstances have a way of taking their toll. The best of men can be . . . changed, in ways they don't understand and we don't recognize. At least, not right away. Do you understand what I am trying to tell you?"

"Yes, sir."

"All right. Please crank up the generator. And stand by, I might need some help here."

"I'm sorry, sir, but I have to go. I am leading the team at Old Crow. I'll get someone else to help with the generator."

Schevardnadze looked startled. "But . . . are you sure that's wise? Approaching the village, I mean?"

"No, sir, I'm not. But I have to carry out my orders."

Schevardnadze sighed. "Very well. But please be careful, Lieutenant."

"Yes, sir. Thank you, sir."

Ekizian snapped a brisk salute. This time he stepped outside. Schevardnadze waited. A few moments later the generator coughed. Light was restored to the interior of the half-track.

Disconnecting the damaged cables from the transmitter, he quickly replaced them with others stripped from one of the less important instruments. He snugged the coaxial F-connectors to the chassis and sat back for a moment.

Taking a deep breath, Schevardnadze flipped the main power switch. The familiar dance of LEDs signaled the internal check routine. When the sequence had been repeated twice, the ready light glowed softly, its red eye staring steadily back at the major.

Turning to the frequency of one of the Cosmos satellites, he goosed the gain and waited. A steady hum filled the half-track. Everything seemed normal, but the hum was too loud and there was no signal. Lifting the case, he peered inside again, using the flashlight to clear out the shadows. One by one he worked his way through the sequence of chips, pressing each one firmly, hoping one had been loosened by the concussion.

The next to last chip felt loose under his finger. He pressed harder, wiggling his fingertip to persuade it firmly into its socket. Suddenly the familiar sound from the Cosmos filled the room. A generator broadcast a constant tone for regulation purposes. It was used by Soviet ships all over the globe to calibrate their electronic gear. It was the best way to provide a constant that was universally accessible. Each satellite in the complex Cosmos network broadcast the same tone, insuring total communications compatibility.

Retuning to the backup frequency, he was instantly rewarded by the sound of the second signal.

Remembering the last thing he'd picked up before the explosion, Schevardnadze hurriedly tuned to the frequency of the unit's walkie-talkies. He was sure he'd heard something, a human voice.

He only hoped it wasn't too late for Karpov. And for Old Crow.

CHAPTER 14

The small buildings of Old Crow looked even more forlorn in the darkness. Huddling together against the cold and swirling snow, their weathered exteriors seemed to soak up the darkness, as if they had surrendered to some hidden enemy, preferring a life of subjection to none at all.

Colonel Arkady Borlov stood on a low rise outside of town, surveying the scene through binoculars. He counted fifteen buildings, mostly homes. A general store that also functioned as infirmary, post office, hotel, and saloon was the only building taller than a single story.

Soft light glowed in a handful of windows, but most of the buildings were completely dark. Borlov grinned in satisfaction. There would be no resistance and no trouble. He hadn't wanted to spare the men to ride herd on a bunch of bearded savages in flannel shirts, but even Chertok had argued that bloodshed was unnecessary. He had thought it hypocritical of the *spetznaz*, but the mission came first. So he told Schevardnadze they would simply round up the villagers and isolate them until their mission was complete.

Nestled in a small depression in the hilly terrain, barely worthy of the word *valley*, Old Crow was going to be easy

97

pickings. Looking through the dark gray night, he waited for the signal. A second unit was circling around behind the hamlet. Dispatched to the opposite hill, they would move in as soon as he gave the command. It was a simple maneuver, almost elegant in its economy, almost a textbook exercise. The chances of anything going wrong were virtually nil. He was suddenly glad he had decided to accompany the assault unit. Ekizian was a good young officer, but right now he was younger than he was good.

His walkie-talkie dangled from a leather strap in the receive mode. Borlov reached absently to wipe a few stray flakes of snow from the binocular objectives. He left behind a damp smear. It was like looking through a window on a rainy night. He hadn't felt such tranquillity before an operation since his first tour of Afghanistan.

Borlov looked at the men arrayed behind him. Sitting patiently on their sleds, they might have been getting ready for an afternoon outing in the country. With fifteen men behind him, and another fifteen on the opposite hill, he had nothing to worry about.

Growing impatient, Borlov dropped the glasses and hoisted the handset. He fumbled through the mitten to switch to transmit. He whispered hoarsely, as if the town could hear him, "Schevardnadze, where the hell are you? We're waiting."

"Almost ready, Colonel."

Borlov grunted. He had thought it a nice wrinkle to put Schevardnadze in command of the second unit. Might as well get some real use out of the man. Science was all well and good, but it was men and experience that won wars. A few seconds later the handset crackled.

"We're in position, Colonel."

"Good. Now remember, the men are not to fire unless fired upon."

"And if they are?"

"They won't be. Don't worry about it, Major."

"Yes, sir."

"All right, we go in thirty seconds. You know what to do. On my mark . . ." He paused to watch the sweep hand of his field watch. At five seconds he started counting. ". . . three

. . . two . . ." The soft rumble of the sleds behind him grew restive. He felt the floorboards of his own sled begin to shudder. ". . . one . . . now!"

Down below, Jason Mackenzie stood on his porch, a shovel in one hand. His heavy woolen coat was open, a scarf dangling freely around his neck. The scraping of the shovel had been interrupted by something out in the darkness. The first time he'd stopped shoveling, he had listened for several minutes, but when the sound wasn't repeated, he had returned to the snow removal with a shrug. Now, leaning on the shovel, he was convinced he'd heard something.

Mackenzie stabbed the shovel into a mound of fresh snow piled to the left of the raw wood porch. He stepped out into the snow with a crunch. The sound was there all right, and getting louder. It sounded like a small engine, but the noise was richer than it should have been and more resonant. Besides, no one from the village would be out on a night like this. And, sure as hell, they weren't going to get visitors at one o'clock in the morning. Not without some warning over the radio.

Advancing into the darkness a few steps, Mackenzie strained his ears. The sound seemed to be coming from two directions. He walked into the broad open space in front of Mackenzie's General Store. Instinctively he flicked the scarf over his shoulder, drawing it tighter around his neck.

Then he saw the lights, two dozen small points, in two swarms, rolling toward him. He wiped his eyes with the rough leather of his gloves, then started running toward the store. His boots thumped on the rough planks of the porch, and he banged in through the heavy door, slamming it roughly back against the wall with a hollow thud.

He leaned over the counter and grabbed his Winchester .30-30 carbine. Fumbling under the lip of the Formica countertop, he felt a box of shells, grabbed it, and stuffed it into his pocket. The carbine, he knew, was loaded. It always was.

Things got rough in a hurry up here. The nearest lawman was three hundred miles away, and he had too much ground to cover and too little interest in covering it. People mostly looked out for themselves and, if it wasn't too much trouble, for one another. Jason had a feeling he was going to need help. A crack, nearly inaudible in the wind, echoed from the far end of the town. Something slammed into the packed snow at his feet and buried itself in the frozen crust. He didn't have to dig it out to know what it was.

He began to shout, hoping to raise some of his neighbors. Dropping to one knee, he drew a bead on the nearest of the charging lamps. He didn't know whether to fire or not. While he deliberated, he heard a door slam. He looked in the direction of the noise and noticed Rich Silverbird, the town's oddball and resident Indian, hauling suspenders up over his shoulders.

"Jace, what the hell's going on?"

"I don't know, Rick, but you better get a gun and get out here. Whoever it is just took a shot at me. Make some noise, too, and get us some help."

Silverbird turned to go back inside, stopping to clang the heavy iron bell hanging over his front porch. The bell was a relic and served any purpose for which one might conceivably need to make a racket, everything from a fire to a party. The racket seemed to reverberate off the few walls in town.

Mackenzie noticed several lights flicker on, then turned his attention back to the advancing swarms. They buzzed now, like angry insects. Sweeping down the hills at either end of the town, they seemed bent on meeting in its middle like the ranchers and sodbusters in countless Westerns he'd seen. Something told him it might be just as violent in a few minutes.

Borlov, halfway down the hill, his sled in the lead, noticed the sudden flurry of lights. He debated calling a halt, then, spurred on by the sense that this was one uncomplicated confrontation he could win for a pleasant change, he leaned in to shout in his driver's ear.

"Faster. They must have heard us."

On the opposite slope, Schevardnadze, too, noticed the sudden activity. Raising his right arm, he slowed his detachment, coasting to a halt seventy-five yards from the bottom of the hill. Convinced that Borlov, too, would stop, he watched the swirling lights across the top of the houses. But when the pace quickened, he realized Borlov wasn't going to give up so easily.

Reluctantly he gave the command to resume their descent. The sleds behind him roared loudly, as if to make up for lost time.

Mackenzie, still on one knee, redrew his bead. He debated whether to fire a warning shot or whether he should fire at all. Maybe he should wait until he found out what was going on. But he knew, even before considering the possibility, that it was the wrong thing to do.

He squeezed off a shot, straining his ears for some change in the sound. The report of the Winchester was ripped away by the wind, like a scrap of tissue paper. He knew it hadn't reached the men pouring down the hillside. He levered another round into the chamber, aimed quickly, and fired again. This time the crack seemed to travel farther as the wind stilled momentarily, then picked up with renewed intensity. The snow swirling in the street kept hiding and unveiling the lights, now growing rapidly larger.

Several men ran toward him, and he took his eyes off the fireflies long enough to realize that several of his neighbors, also armed, had joined him in the streets.

"What the hell is going on?" Silverbird asked, dropping down beside him.

"I don't know. I popped a couple at them, but nothing happened. I don't know who they are, but there's a passel of them. Both ends of town."

Silverbird turned to look over his shoulder. He gestured with one hand, and a few of the others turned to face the opposite end of Main Street, the one and only street in Old Crow.

The first sleds hit the flat. The lights rushed toward the handful of men in the middle of the street. Mackenzie fired again. This time he was rewarded by the disappearance of one of the lights. Following his lead, the others began to fire their own weapons. A motley assortment of carbines, shotguns, and deer rifles cracked brittlely in the wind. The sound, as if chilled by the cold, seemed to snap and shatter, like so many ice crystals tinkling to the ground.

Mackenzie looked over his shoulder and realized that the other group of lights, which had stopped momentarily, had picked up speed to make up lost ground. They, too, were on the flat, ready for a straight run down the center of the village. So far there had been no response from the visitors.

Borlov ordered his detachment into a shallow arc, his sled at the point. He slowed to a crawl while the formation developed on either side of him. He noted with satisfaction that Schevardnadze, after a momentary hesitation, was following suit.

Silverbird, swiveling his gaze from one end of the street to the other, immediately understood that they were doomed if they held their ground. Attracted by the firing, every man in the village had now rushed into the street. They were all armed but only in the ignorance of what they were facing.

Mackenzie grasped their dilemma at nearly the same instant. "We have to get out of the street," he yelled. "Rick, take half of the men up the alley to the left. I'll take the others to the opposite side."

Mackenzie knew he and Rick were the only two men in the village with any combat experience. The others, occasional hunters and fisherman, knew the terrain but lacked any useful sense of how to exploit it for their own protection.

He gathered his handful around him and watched Rick lead his men into a narrow opening between two low wooden buildings. When they were out of sight, he waved his own men into the wide side yard of the general store. A large, heavily loaded truck, its tires half buried in the drifting snow, stood close to the side of the store.

For a moment he considered using it to move the men, then realized it would be easily outmaneuvered by the sleds at either end of the town. If they were going to get out of this jam, it was going to be on foot.

Borlov, satisfied that both halves of his force were in position, barked the order to move ahead. Schevardnadze responded, but his words were lost in a crackle of electrical static. Borlov didn't bother to ask for a resend. In this array it didn't matter whether Schevardnadze advanced or not. As long as he held his ground, he would be the anvil on which Borlov could hammer out his latest victory.

Taking up positions against the flimsy wooden buildings, Mackenzie's men prepared for the charge they knew would be coming. Cover was minimal. The opening between buildings was so broad, men facing in one direction would have their backs exposed to fire coming from the other end of town.

He ran to the truck, hoping the key was still in the ignition. He sighed when he caught the glint of its chain as he climbed into the cab. He turned the key, pumped the accelerator, and cranked it up. The engine, sluggish in the cold, groaned reluctantly for a second, then whined as the starter insisted. The engine coughed, then died. He pumped again, hoping he hadn't flooded the carburetor.

This time when he turned the key, the engine rumbled and held. He threw the truck in gear and backed it up until it stood between the men and the street. Its high carriage wouldn't protect them completely, but some cover was better than none.

Jumping down out of the cab, he ran to the men on the opposite wall. The first chatter of gunfire cracked in the distance. Whoever they were, they were coming.

Now.

The weapons were automatic—of that he was certain. Rick and his men were long gone. He hoped Rick was working along the back side of the town, positioning himself to pick targets of opportunity. Not knowing how many men they were up against was a handicap. If they could cut the odds a bit in the first few minutes, they might have a chance. If not, well . . .

Suddenly a roar swelled at the far end of the village. With a concerted whine, several of the sleds jumped forward. Headlong down Main Street they came. A deadly hail of fire chewed at the wooden wall behind him, slammed into the truck, and ripped ice and snow from the ground all around him.

He turned in time to see the truck vanish in a ball of fire. Ungodly screams ripped the night open as if to let in the orange light dancing on the walls. He peeked out and saw four sleds, two men on each, roaring straight toward him. He opened up with the Winchester. His first shot slammed into the driver of the lead sled. A dark star exploded on the man's white parka, and he tumbled backward.

The sled careened out of control, veered to the left, and slammed into a wall. Mackenzie pumped two more slugs and saw the sled rise on a bright yellow stem, then fall shudderingly back to the ground. Its fuel burned quickly, leaving charred wreckage behind. The hot metal sizzled in the pool of melt-water against the wall. The building itself, splashed with the fuel, had begun to burn. Momentarily frightened, the drivers of the other sleds skidded to a halt, then backed into a tight circle.

Firing as fast as he could crank the lever, Mackenzie emptied the magazine. Two of his companions, emboldened by the delay, charged into the open. Sam Waters, a hulk of a man, roared triumphantly, and let go with his 12-gauge, both barrels barking at once. The cloud of double ought buzzed across the windshield of the front sled. It smashed the driver's skull, then chewed it loose, leaving a gory stump behind, gouting dark blood. The other man, though he had been less directly hit, was just as dead.

Sam stumbled, and as he fell, Jason heard the chatter of a machine gun farther up the street. He ducked out and down, flattening himself in the snow. Sam tried to get up as Jason watched helplessly. The machine gunner, like a cat toying with a mouse, walked his fire up the block, catching Sam up the middle, just as he regained his balance.

The battle suddenly changed character. The familiar whine of shoulder-launched missiles screamed down the block. In three quick bursts, like erupting mushrooms, the three buildings directly across the street ballooned outward and were gone. Burning rubble littered the snowy street. Looking up the block, Jason watched the thin, smoky trails of the missiles come unraveled in the wind.

Jason crawled backward, yanking his head behind the wall just as the machine gun opened up again. Two sleds flashed by in a blur. Jason rolled and pumped three .30-30 slugs from the Winchester, but he fired wildly, and they slammed harm-lessly into the stunted wreckage across the street.

Alone in the open, Mackenzie half crawled and half ran

toward the rear of the building. A low rumble erupted behind him, and he turned to see a sled skid to a halt in the center of the yard. Desperately Jason dived to the left, bringing the Winchester up as he landed on his elbows in a snowbank. He sighted quickly and fired once. The building to his left vanished in a cloud of splinters as he fired again. The sled, both occupants dead, idled at a low rumble.

Getting to his feet, Jason sprinted forward. He tossed the dead driver to the snow, dropped into the seat, and gunned the sled, fumbling with its unfamiliar controls. The sled shot forward, and Jason sped straight toward the steep hill behind the buildings.

As he hit the incline he gave the lolling corpse beside him a shove. The dead man rolled to the side, and Jason, with a sudden inspiration, reached out and hauled him back in. He aimed for a stand of scrubby pines on the ridge. He had extinguished the light and slowed to avoid hitting anything in the dark.

He yanked the dead man's weapon from his shoulder. With a shock he realized it was a Kalashnikov AK-47. Turning his attention back to the corpse, he searched the man's pockets. The wallet confirmed what he couldn't believe. The man was a Russian soldier.

Kneeling in the snow, his mouth open, too slack to close, he looked down at the smoking ruins below him. As he watched, the roof of his store ballooned up and out, then was obliterated by a cloud of oily smoke.

Jason Mackenzie was alone, with the Russian Army tearing his town to pieces.

CHAPTER 15

Tran Cao sat as if mesmerized. Watching raw data pour in from the Big Bird satellite was normally about as interesting as watching a late-night test pattern.

But tonight, the pattern held him. His neck muscles grew taut, the tension spreading across his shoulders and down his back. Suddenly his hands danced on the switch bank. Pulling a large hunk of the most recent transmission, he dumped it to the Cray supercomputer and ordered an immediate translation.

The spools of the secondary data bank began to spin as his patch was selected and cross-fed to a virgin tape. Patching the slice into the Cray, Tran flipped on the high-resolution monitor and waited for the decryption conversion to be completed. When the spools grew still, he punched the feed switch and rolled his stool over, close to the monitor.

The first flickering image was nondescript. Night photos, even infrared, were not much to look at. The cloud cover kept the clarity at a minimal level. Contours of the upper half of the Yukon territory were discernible, helped by imagination and Tran's knowledge of the topography. He grabbed a ring binder from a shelf under the monitor, flipped its pages hurriedly, then, finding the page he needed, slapped it flat on the table. Running his finger down a column of twelve-digit numbers, he located the one he wanted near the bottom.

Another dance on the switch bank and he had a superimposition. Feeding the raw data into an overlay of a clear night shot of the same terrain, the background features took a quantum leap in clarity. Then, cutting the feed into frame analogs, he watched a slo-mo sequence. The Bluefish River, a band of silver in the lower left-hand corner of the monitor, shimmered and flashed as the frames played through.

What made him sit up and take notice was a sudden flurry of small smears, within thirty miles of Luke's last location. Playing it back at higher speed, he recognized the smears for what they were: hot spots . . . explosions.

Feeding the Cray an "enhance" command, he replayed, this time in slo-mo again. The heightened clarity imposed by the monstrous machine forced his breath out of his chest in a small explosion. For a second he couldn't breathe.

Tran punched in a set of coordinates, then backed up and asked for a close-up look. He replayed the same sequence. Checking his atlas, he confirmed his guess. The explosions, low-grade but still significant, were centered in Old Crow, the Yukon Territory. He rolled back to check his log, knowing, but out of habit wanting to double-check, that Luke had been fairly close.

Tran dumped the image into an analytical program, then asked for a hard copy of the readout. The program, which he had written three years before and which had immediately been appropriated by the National Security Agency, enabled him to estimate, with a margin of error a hair under five percent, the force of the explosion.

He ran the program, then sat back and watched the printer clack. The paper fairly screamed through the high-speed dot matrix as each separate detonation was tracked, peaked out, then fixed in immutable print. Originally designed to monitor nuclear explosions, the program had proved capable of handling light artillery, as well as some even smaller weapons. The program charted a number of variables, including rate of detonation, degree of randomness, average explosive force, and total explosive force. In this case the result was a numerical analog of a firefight as minutely detailed as a Howard Cosell play-by-play. Fortunately it was more useful, not to mention enlightening.

The program had a soft bottom, and Tran himself wasn't sure how large something had to be in order to be picked up. There was a noise factor that he could estimate, but he had never tried to fix the lower limit. A LAW rocket would show, possibly a grenade, but he wasn't certain of that. The important thing was that the program was reliable and had no ceiling. Something might be too small to be picked up, but nothing was too large to fit. Not that it really mattered. Small was never small enough, and large was too damn large.

Ripping the paper from the printer, Tran quickly scrutinized the results of his analysis. There had been no mistake. Something like a small war had gone on, not twenty minutes ago.

Tran cranked up his transmitter and entered the proper code. He drummed his fingers while he waited. Examining the numbers while he waited, he counted no fewer than thirty detonations of .0002-kiloton size. Small potatoes by nuclear standards, but unless the polar bears and elk had moved into modern weapons, men were killing each other not too far from Luke's last location.

After what seemed like an eternity, Tran heard Luke's flinty rasp on the comm link.

"Got something for me, old buddy?"

"Anybody shooting at you?"

"No. Nobody here but us chickens. Why?"

"Because I just picked up a firefight. At Old Crow. How close is that?"

"Wait a minute."

Tran heard the rustle of stiff paper. The clarity was remarkable, even if you knew the technology involved. Tran sometimes thought it was this childlike wonderment in himself that made him so good at what he did. No matter how often he twiddled dials and read infrared feeds, it still amazed him. A moment later Luke was back, and Tran pushed the wonderment aside.

"Well?"

"By the map, I make it twenty miles or so. Why? What's going on?"

"I'm not sure. It was pretty noisy in Old Crow a half hour ago. Looks like a real shoot-out."

"We haven't seen anything. No contact with anybody, not since we got here. It's been snowing, mostly. Hard to get around in, at least for a child of the Sunbelt, like me."

"With all due respect, Luke, you were never a child."

"At heart I am. Honest."

"I think you better take a look. If there's something going on there, you ought to know about it."

"You pick up any radio transmissions from the area, Tran?"

"I haven't had a chance to check that out. Wanted to let you know right away."

"I don't think it could be Ivan. He's been sitting pretty steady for a while now. We got him locked on. There's been a couple of short stabs, but they were reconnaissance. Ben's even seen them."

"Don't be so sure, Luke. If they've got a heavy transmitter, that would mask some smaller stuff, recon transmits and that sort of thing. Who the hell knows what they might be up to. Or where."

"Okay, look, I'll have somebody take a peek. We're waiting for Calvin to get back from dropping the C-5. Maybe Ben can run over and have a look. It's not a long haul by motor-sled."

"Okay. I'll check for low-level radio and get back to you. Stay near the set, all right?"

"Got my feet up and the coffee on. Don't worry."

Tran signed off, knowing Luke was probably busting his ass.

CHAPTER 16

Malcolm Conroy was having trouble getting some time alone. Wandering off into the night wasn't something he could easily explain. He stood in the doorway, nervously puffing on an English Oval. When the butt was down to the nub, he tossed it out into the snow through the door, cracked open just enough to admit the dead cigarette.

He flipped open the stiff cardboard box and picked another. Conroy rolled the cylinder contemplatively between thumb and forefinger. Deep in concentration, he didn't hear the footsteps behind him. He stuck the new cigarette between his lips, canting it to one side, the way he remembered Bogart doing it. As he raised the lighter he was startled by the hissing flare of a match off to the left.

"Can I grub one from you?" Calvin Steeples asked.

"Huh? Oh . . . sure." Conroy reached back into his pocket for the flat box, flipped it open, and held it toward the newcomer.

Steeples fumbled in the box, stymied by the odd shape of the cigarettes. Finally getting a grip on one, he stuck it into his mouth, squinted, and withdrew it. Holding it toward the dim light coming from behind him, he leaned toward his hand.

"You make these yourself?"

"What?"

"You roll these weeds yourself? They funny-looking. They tobacco?"

"Of course. They're imported. English."

"Yeah, but are they any good?"

"Oh, quite."

" 'Quite'? You English too?"

"Certainly not."

"Then how come you don't talk like somebody ain't English? That what they teach you to sound like in the Ivy League?"

"Look. I was kind enough to give you the cigarette. Now, would you please go someplace and smoke it?"

"Touchy bastard, ain't you. You should try to be more sociable, sport. Somebody likely to think you nervous about something. We wouldn't want that, now would we?"

"What an absurd thing to suggest! What could I have to be nervous about?"

"Well, listen here. You CIA boys are not exactly noted for straight shooting, not in any sense of the phrase. I just thought I'd let you know that we know there ain't no reason to trust you. At least, no further than I can throw this truck."

"I resent that. It's impertinent and offensive."

"Uh-huh. Well, see, I'm kind of well known for my impertinence. But it don't matter. You can add it to your report next time you call home."

Conroy spun around to face Steeples for the first time. "What are you going on about? What report? I'm simply here as an observer, a liaison, that's all. From the Defense Department."

"Right. And Beethoven is just a piano player." Steeples opened the door and stepped outside, then lobbed a parting shot over his shoulder. "See you at the phone booth."

He walked several steps into the dark before turning to see whether Conroy was still there. The door banged shut as he did, and Steeples laughed. He broke into a trot and covered the distance to the makeshift command post in a dozen strides. Pushing aside the flap, he slipped into the tent. The kerosene heater glowed a dull orange through its wide-open grate. Steeples knelt in front of it and rubbed his hands together, trying to restore some circulation.

"Better bring in the brass monkey, boss. It's cold out there."

Luke grunted. "I want the weather, I can turn on the TV."

"Not up here, you can't."

"What do you think?"

"I don't know, Luke. You're right about one thing. Conroy is one nervous little dude. But I don't know whether he's got something up his sleeve or they grow them like that back East."

"He say anything at all?"

"Nothing useful. But he sure as hell is skittish. How come you think he might be leaking?"

"I don't think he is. I'm just afraid he might be. What I can't figure out is how he can contact anybody without us seeing him. I got a funny feeling that's why he's here. Because if it isn't, then I don't have a clue why he's here at all. He's not the typical cowboy. And if there's one thing we don't need, it's an analyst."

"So?"

"So why's he here?"

Steeples shrugged his shoulders. "Maybe they sent him along for seasoning. Or maybe they figure it's better he's in our hair than in theirs. I would bet the farm he gets old real quick."

"If that was all, they'd just sit him at a desk way off in the corner or bounce him altogether. Unless he's some senator's nephew."

"Come on, Luke. Think about it. If he was your nephew, would you admit it?"

Luke laughed. "I guess not. But he's so tight, he squeaks, doesn't he?"

"Want me to lean on him a little harder? Maybe I could put one of them Mick twins on each shoulder, hold him down, like paperweights."

"No. But keep an eye on him, would you? Let me know the least little thing that doesn't seem kosher."

"What do I know about kosher?"

"So learn."

Before Steeples could respond, the radio squawked. Luke grabbed the mike and squeezed the transmit button. "Tran? That you?"

The voice sounded far away but still clear enough that distance didn't disguise the scorn. "Who else would it be?"

"What have you got for us?"

"Trouble, for sure. You hear from Ben yet?"

"No, not yet."

"Well, you won't like what he's got to tell you. I think you better hotfoot it for Old Crow. Now."

"What's going on?"

"Try World War III."

"What are you talking about?"

"The question is who? And the answer is Ivan. Say the secret word and look out for the duck."

"What the hell are you talking about, Tran?"

"I screened the night's pickup. There was more than a little conversation in Russian, not more than two hours ago. Close enough to Old Crow to be right in the heart of downtown. However big that is."

"You're telling me there was a firefight and that Russians were involved."

"Not just involved, Luke. Judging by the weapons I picked up, they were doing most of the shooting. The serious shooting, anyway."

"That's ridiculous. We put them twenty miles north of Old Crow. Besides, there's no way they would risk that. Not here. Not in Canada."

"I don't know whether they'd risk it. But I know they did it, risk or not. And you'd do well to remember that risk is a relative thing. They may not see it as a risk at all. But I'll tell you one thing . . . if they're as sensible as we are, the stakes are pretty damn high. I don't know what was in that nose cone, but they sure as hell want it back."

"They still there?"

"I can't tell. The next dump isn't scheduled for another two hours. I can ask the NSA boys to push it up, but I better have a good reason. The one I already have is better kept secret, don't you think?"

"Damn right. Until we know what the hell is going on, don't breathe a word."

"Check. Want me to put a rush on the intel? I can probably think of a good reason without spilling the beans."

"Yeah, Tran. Do it. But make sure somebody's on the horn at all times. I might need some quick answers. I'll check in as soon as I hear from Ben. That should be in a half hour or so."

"You better hope that Indian doesn't go off half cocked. I can't tell how many Russkies there are, but you can bet it's a few dozen. No way they would chance anything less."

Stiles Moreland leaned back in his large, overstuffed suede chair. He webbed his hands behind his head and propped his feet on the dark mahogany of his uncluttered desk. "What have you got so far?"

"As near as we can figure, there's a contingent of approximately one hundred men, and significant hardware, in the Old Crow vicinity."

"What about Conroy? Have we heard from him?"

"Not yet."

The Director of Central Intelligence rocked a bit in the chair, leaving his hands linked. A man more remarkable for his easy manner with the media than any other single quality, Moreland was not held in high esteem by career intelligence people.

David Naughton, the Deputy Director for Plans, was no exception. They had been classmates at Harvard, but the kinship stopped there. Naughton was rough-edged and sharp-tongued. Where Moreland was all style and politesse, Naughton was gruff to the point of rudeness.

Even physical appearance opposed them. Moreland wore two-thousand-dollar suits from Brooks Brothers, the right tie over the right shirt. "Impeccably attired" invariably accompanied the frequent references to him in the society columns.

His thick black hair, slightly waved and just hinting at gray, seemed never to grow and was impervious to the wind.

Naughton was anything but smooth. A twice broken nose gave him the face of a plug-ugly. He had a disposition to match. His broad shoulders waged war on anything with sleeves. He had sandy, thinning hair, and his pale—some said baleful—gray eyes sat in rough cheeks, untroubled by smile wrinkles.

"I think we can wait a bit, don't you?" Moreland rocked uneasily in the capacious chair. He was never quite comfortable dealing with the DDP. Naughton had not been his choice, but he was too much the gentleman to push for his own candidate. And Naughton, the only career man under consideration, had been the favorite son of the rest of the Agency. Recent presidents had been less than traditionlists in choosing the DCI, and most observers felt some sense of continuity was essential.

Naughton was it. A block of granite in a stone wall, he kept the troops if not happy, at least in line. Considering the question, he cracked huge knuckles in his lap. Moreland kept peeking, expecting to find a glaze of calcine dust on the DDP's rumpled trousers.

When he finally got around to answering, he wasn't sure Moreland remembered the question, but he plunged ahead. "No, I don't think we can afford to wait. NSA puts some Soviet troops on the scene. There has been some shooting, we don't know how much or by whom, but we'll have that soon."

"You don't think these people Defense has hired are going to start a war, do you? That would be unfortunate."

Naughton laughed in spite of himself. "Unfortunate? I guess you could say that. But no, Deadly Force is unlikely to do anything foolish. The honcho, Simpson, was an analyst with the Company a few years ago. He's impatient but not a hothead."

"What should we do?"

"I think we ought to contact Conroy and get a firsthand report. All this high-tech stuff is so much window dressing. I don't like to rely on it."

"Won't that blow Conroy's cover?"

"If Luke Simpson is as sharp as I think he is, Conroy never had a cover. He'd make him in a dark alley with one eye closed."

"So, all right. Get to Conroy. But don't compromise him unnecessarily."

Naughton hesitated.

"You disagree?"

"No, I don't. But I don't think we ought to stop there."

"What do you suggest?"

"I think we ought to mount our own operation. At least get a team within striking distance."

"Striking distance? Are you talking about another one of your cowboy operations? We still haven't lived the last one down, David."

"That wasn't my fault. All those media friends of yours did us in on that one. You ought to keep your distance."

"We have an image that needs a little buffing, David." Moreland blew on his immaculate nails and rubbed them on his sleeve. He examined them closely and, satisfied, looked at his subordinate. "I'm not sure we can afford another debacle."

"Are you sure we can afford to let Ivan get his garbage back?"

"David, we don't even know what's in it. What's the urgency here?"

"We don't know what's in it. That's the urgency, Stiles. If it's important enough for the Soviets to violate the territorial integrity of our closest ally, then it's important enough for us to get involved. I thought we had agreed on that up front."

"Yes, we did. But to what extent? We didn't even consider anything like what you're proposing."

"Stiles, look . . . NSA is getting piles of elint, all of which suggests something hot is going down. How hot, we don't know. The question is, should we wait until we do know and get caught with our thumbs up our collective ass, or should we assume a worst-case scenario and take steps to contain the damage. I don't think the answer is that difficult."

Moreland tilted farther back in his chair. The pause, as both he and Naughton knew, was purely theatrical.

"All right, David. Do it your way. But check with me before you take any drastic action. All I'm authorizing at this point is gearing up. You are not to go any further without my approval."

"Understood." Naughton left without saying good-bye.

Moreland didn't even notice.

CHAPTER 17

Ben Sanchez left his sled with the engine running. The slope in front of him was steep but not insurmountable. He knelt to slip on a pair of lightweight plastic snowshoes, Teflon-coated to reduce sticking. There's at least one virtue to progress, he thought.

The crest of the hill glowed softly with a pale orange corona. The smell of burning wood was acrid and strong. He knew what he'd see when he reached the crest of the hill, but Luke wanted an eyewitness account. And that's what he'd get.

The wind was blocked by the hillside, and the going was easier than Ben had anticipated. Small shrubs poked out of the snow, their thick, flat needles reminding him of cactus. He slogged up the hill, leaning forward to facilitate the climb.

As he neared the top of the hill the corona became a cloud. Mixed with the overpowering smell of incinerated wood was something stronger, something familiar . . . the stench of cordite and the bite of burning petroleum products, mostly kerosene.

Just below the ridge line, Ben turned to look back down the slope. He could no longer see the outline of his sled among the sparsely scattered trees. Cocking his ear, he listened. For a second he thought he could hear the engine throbbing, but the wind picked up and the impression was ripped away.

Ben climbed the last dozen steps to the top of the hill. The snow was broken and clumped, as if someone, or something, had passed by within the last couple of hours. Between the still falling snow and the wind-driven ground snow, it was hard to say for sure.

He stood on the crest and looked down on the remains of Old Crow.

Most of the buildings had been leveled. Broken stumps of studs and joists stuck out at odd angles. They were blurry-edged and charred black. Smoke still gushed from most of the charred structures, and snow hissed as it fell onto the coals.

The orange glow was centered in the remains of a large van. It had been shattered and split open like a vegetable can. Its contents, apparently fifty-five-gallon drums, still burned furiously. Several of the large containers had been thrown free, probably by the blast that had leveled the vehicle, and the snow around the wreckage was gone, either melted by the flame or dissolved by the liquid. "Probably both," Ben muttered as he surveyed the wreckage.

He dropped to his belly and watched. The place seemed deserted, but he realized how reckless he had been by standing, outlined against the gray sky in his white parka. After what seemed a motionless eternity, Ben decided the place was as deserted as it seemed.

Working his way down the front of the hill, he moved from bush to bush. They didn't provide much cover, but he felt as if he ought to take some precautions, anyway.

As the hill flattened out, the cover, such as it was, disappeared altogether, and Ben abandoned the pretense. Fully erect but moving cautiously, he approached the nearest charred foundation. Small swirls of smoke coiled up and away on the wind. By all appearances, it had been a house. Spartanly furnished at best, but someone's home nevertheless. Ben stepped carefully over the saw-toothed charcoal stubble that had been one wall and walked through the blackened ruins.

A crash behind him made him whirl. His eyes refocused in

time to see the rear of the building, less severely damaged than the front and sides, teeter precariously then, in slow motion, complete the outward journey initiated by the blast that had brought the house down.

Ben felt the eerie sensation of eyes boring into him. Instinctively he ducked down, taking cover behind a ruined metal closet leaning out over the foundation. He tried to fix the source of the feeling, but it was too vague even for his heightened sixth sense. He jumped over the low remains of the wall, landing with a thud in a soggy snowdrift. His boots squished as he sprinted to the next building.

Diving into a mound of snow at the base of the wall, he squirmed around to survey the hillside behind him. Dark masses of shadow, the bushes, were the only thing in sight. The orange glow from the blazing drums colored everything a garish, circus tint. In front of him a broad, deserted street, full of swirling snow, separated him from the second, and only other, line of buildings. Most of them, like the one on his side of the street, had been leveled. At the far end, to his left, stood three buildings seemingly untouched by whatever had happened here.

Ben scrutinized the street. Its center was rutted deeply, by what he couldn't tell. Getting to his feet, he dashed into the opening, diving to his stomach at the center of the street. He rolled into one rut, his body parallel to the street, and examined the depression, wider than his body. He scraped at the snow with one mitten, then blew the loose flakes aside. The telltale rectangles of a heavy tread were unmistakable. Offset, on the inner edge of the rut, he found the herringbone pattern of heavy-duty tires. "A half-track," he whispered. Then, conscious of the soft articulation, he wondered whether he was talking to someone he couldn't see, or fearful that someone might overhear him.

He was in the nearer rut. Parallel to it, and between it and the companion left by the half-track, were smaller lines, much shallower, like those of skis. He realized immediately they had been left by a motor-sled like his own. Poking his head up as far as he dared, he spotted several other sets of similar lines. He flashed to the Russian sled he'd seen, and the APCs. Could they have come this far, to wreck a village that posed no threat to them? If so, why?

He wanted to get to the opposite side of the street. For some reason he couldn't explain, he was convinced he'd find something important there, something that would explain what he'd already seen and only dimly understood. Climbing to his knees, using his rifle as a crutch, he stood in a crouch, sprinting to the relative shelter of the far buildings. He felt a little foolish, like a lonely kid playing a solitary game of war.

But he wasn't alone.

And he knew it.

The wind died suddenly. Ben strained his ears into the darkness, trying to pierce it for any clue that would help explain the mystery. The wind came with renewed force, and the chance was gone. The eerie howl seemed to split and fragment on the broken walls, as if chewed by blackened teeth. Ben reached for his radio, then changed his mind. He wasn't ready to call in yet. He had nothing definite to report.

Unable to shake the feeling that he wasn't alone, Ben stood. If anybody was there, let him come. Ben walked out onto the middle of the street again. The orange flames still danced, but their energy was flagging. The liquid in the drums was running out. Already one half-upended container had flamed out.

His eye was caught by a mound in the street. Its shape looked unnatural to him. He walked toward the mound, hefting the rifle nervously, as if to reassure himself that he was armed. He prodded at the mound with the toe of one boot. The boot sank in easily, then hit something soft but with a spongy resilience. He scraped at the snow with his foot. A checkered pattern, dark red and black, appeared under a thin crust of melted snow. A shirt.

Ben knelt down and clawed at the snow with both hands. After some furious scraping, he stared at his discovery. The discovery stared back through open, frozen eyes. Sam Waters didn't see him, and Ben Sanchez had seen enough.

He stood up and kicked the snow back over the body of the dead man. The makeshift burial mound glowed softly orange in the dancing glare. Colored shadows spilled down over its far side and vanished in the blue-gray shade at its base. It was time to call in.

Ben inhaled deeply, held the breath a while, then let it out. He turned his back on the corpse and walked toward the flames. The stench of burning kerosene jumped at him. The blackened barrels, gaping like the mouths of several small hells, hissed and sputtered as they spewed smoke and flame into the night. The truck, little more than a charred frame sitting on tireless rims, groaned as it settled a little more deeply into the thawing earth beneath it.

On the far side, between the shell of the truck and that of a large building, he saw something that called to him by its silence. Skirting the hot metal wreckage, he bent to examine clumps of shadow, huddled against the cinder-block foundation of the structure. There were four of them. Darker than the charred ruins, they were nevertheless recognizable: the remains of four men, each curled into a ball, the stockless hull of a rifle or shotgun by each man's side.

Ben crossed himself, exposure to the Catholic missionaries on the reservation surfacing once again, as it occasionally did, always in a time of stress, and always too late to do any good for anyone.

"Rest in peace. Whoever the hell you are," Ben whispered.

Another mound lay in the middle of the opening, a few yards away. He walked toward it, knowing already what it was but needing to confirm it with his eyes. He scraped away the snow, found the thick white parka beneath it, and knew this was something different. Something bright glowed dully in the fur, and Ben brushed again to uncover it . . . a red star, like the one on the sentry's hat.

The young man was a Russian soldier. Tran was right.

Ben stood again, pausing to stare down into the sightless eyes reluctantly, as if, like Snow White's stepmother's magic mirror, they might show him something he didn't wish to see.

Turning his back on the carnage, he walked toward the rear of the building, resisting the urge to break into a run. The plastic snowshoes clacked on the snow, hissing as they slid through the surface, and grabbed onto the crust beneath it. He kept right on walking until he was halfway up the hill.

Across the ruined town he could just make out the hill where his sled still waited. He paused to think, still disoriented by the grisly discovery. Walking backward now, his eyes still scanning the small hamlet from end to end, it seemed to Ben like a ghoulish negative. He had seen countless such villages, their ruined shells smoking against napalm-blackened earth. But this wasn't Vietnam, and the earth was white, the deathly white of an Oriental funeral. Shaking his head, as if in a sudden uncontrollable spasm, Ben closed his eyes and stumbled backward up the slope.

On the crest he fell to his knees. He opened his eyes again and couldn't tear them away. It seemed impossible. How could you get any farther away from superpower politics than this frozen wasteland? And yet, staring him in the face was the incontrovertible proof.

Ben once again yanked out his radio. He looked at it dumbly, as if he didn't recognize it. He thumbed the transmit button, saw the red light flash on, then clicked it off again. Putting the radio back in his pocket, he started to trudge back down the hill. He heard the muffled voice of Luke Simpson calling to him from the pocketed radio but ignored it.

Picking up speed, Ben hit the flat expanse behind the shattered store and walked back past the dead soldier and the grisly shadows at the base of the wall. In the center of the street he ignored the mound concealing Sam Waters and strode up the opposite hill.

On the crest he was tempted to look back. He stopped, as if considering the urge, then shrugged. He pushed on down the hill into the shadows, dimly aware of the orange glow dying behind him. He stepped into his own vacant prints, partially filled with new snow, and followed them to the sled. It was still running, its engine hissing as wet snow fell on its heated housing.

He noticed the small hole melted in the snow by the exhaust pipe. Brushing snow from the seat, he sat down and reached into his pocket for the radio. It felt heavy in his hand. He blew some loose flakes from the speaker grid, depressed the transmit button, and waited for Luke to acknowledge.

The green receiving LED winked, and Luke's voice crackled at him. "Ben, are you all right? Why the hell don't you answer?"

"I'm okay, Luke. Everything's okay."

Ben hesitated, trying to decide whether to report now or wait until he got back. Now was best, because Luke, in all probability, would want an on-site inspection himself. As much as he wanted to pretend he hadn't seen anything, he knew he had no choice. He depressed the transmit button again, saw the light wink on, then went stiff.

He didn't have to look to recognize the unfriendly feel of a high-caliber rifle muzzle pressing on the back of his head. The voice didn't sound any friendlier.

"Hold it right there, Comrade."

CHAPTER 18

"Was that really necessary, Colonel?" Schevardnadze was shaking. Unable to conceal the revulsion in his voice, he decided to give it full expression.

"Regrettably, yes. But it doesn't concern you, Major Schevardnadze. Your responsibilities are specific and, I might add, rather limited. I suggest you tend to them and leave military questions to those best equipped to address them."

"There was nothing military about it. That was outright murder, Colonel Borlov." Schevardnadze pounded his fist into the wall of the truck. "Those people were no threat to us. They were barely armed and certainly not in a position to prevent us from performing our assignment."

"They knew we were here, Major. That was threat enough. You know as well as I do that it was essential to keep our presence here a secret. Once they discovered us, well . . . what would you have me do? Compromise the mission?"

"There had to be another way, dammit!"

Borlov smiled, the very soul of tolerance. "Perhaps. In any case, it hardly matters now, Major."

"Not to you, obviously. But it matters to me. And you

might as well know I feel obligated to report this monstrous act.''

Borlov laughed aloud. "Report it? Report it to whom? And exactly what would you say? That in order to preserve the integrity of a sensitive matter I was forced to take extreme action? I hardly think an eyebrow will be raised at that, Major.''

"We shall see.''

"Very well. If you insist on reporting it, perhaps you can begin with Comrade Captain Chertok. I'm sure he'll be quite interested in what you have to say. Captain?''

The door opened and Chertok stepped in. His features were calm. The eyes, flat as always, skipped from one man to the other and back. He said nothing.

Borlov sat down. "You heard, Captain?''

Chertok nodded.

"Major Schevardnadze takes exception to our conduct in the recent unpleasantness. Perhaps you can help him draft a report.''

"I don't need any help," Schevardnadze snapped.

"Oh, but you will, Major. You most certainly will. And although I'm quite certain he's too modest to tell you this himself, Captain Chertok was the architect of our little maneuver. Who better to help you accurately describe the engagement?''

Schevardnadze looked at Chertok. The captain stood quietly, his hands folded discreetly in front of him. Schevardnadze was stunned. How could he have so badly misread their previous conversation? Borlov continued, but Schevardnadze only half heard him.

"Perhaps you can prepare a draft. I should like to read it over, Major, in order to prepare my defense. Shall we say in one hour? Be quite sure you make clear that we were fired upon first.''

"That's irrelevant, Colonel, and you know it. You planned on destroying the village, anyway.''

"Did I?''

Schevardnadze said nothing, and Borlov pushed on. "And when your report is done, I suggest you do what you were sent here to do, Major. Find that damned rocket. If you are so concerned about the local civilians, the best thing you can do for them is get us out of here as quickly as possible. And I don't think I have to remind you that none of us is leaving here without it. Hmm?''

Schevardnadze stalked out of the command truck. He was halfway to the communications vehicle when he heard footsteps behind him. He stopped but chose not to turn around. He felt a hand on his shoulder. Still, he didn't turn.

"Major, try to understand the colonel's perspective.'' It was Chertok.

"I suppose you had more than a little to do with the attack,'' Schevardnadze mumbled. He was aware how risky it was to talk to anyone about the command decision of a superior officer. Saying anything at all to a *spetznaz* was arguably suicidal.

Chertok didn't respond immediately. Instead he let his hand drop. Schevardnadze turned to face him at last.

"We all have to do things we don't like on occasion.''

"Are you saying you disagree with Colonel Borlov? Or that I should simply accept what happened even though I disagree with it?''

"Both, Comrade. I am saying both.''

"I'm surprised.''

"Don't be. We are all specialists, Major. You kid yourself that your specialty is less . . . brutal . . . than my own. But that is splitting hairs. Murder at one remove, no matter how great the distance, is still murder. Those killed by the missiles you help design are just as dead as those men back there in the snow. Don't deceive yourself about that.''

"I don't, I assure you, Captain Chertok. Maybe I did once but not anymore.''

"I wouldn't let my conscience get in the way here. It is a luxury in the best of times, which these are not.''

"Don't worry about it, Captain. I place as high a value on my head as the next man. But there are limits to how much a man, regardless of the state of his conscience, can be asked to accept. And there are remedies, after all. You know as well as I do that Colonel Borlov is unfit to command this mission.''

"Do I?"

"Of course you do, or you wouldn't be here now."

"Let us accept that premise, for the sake of argument. What would you have me do? You know the penalty for mutiny. Have you forgotten the sailors at Kronstadt? That, too, was a case of conscience. It proved fatal for the afflicted."

"That was fifty years ago. Things have changed."

"Would it were so. But things are not always what they seem. As a scientist, you should know that better than most men."

"What do you mean?"

"You know there are representatives of the Committee for State Security in this detachment."

"Yes."

"But you don't know who they are."

Schevardnadze looked at Chertok closely for the first time. He became conscious of the oddity of the conversation. It seemed as if Chertok were trying to tell him something, something Chertok thought should have been obvious to him. But the point eluded him. He turned to look back at Borlov's truck.

He was baffled. "What are you trying to say?" Schevardnadze asked.

"Think about it." Without another word Chertok stepped past him and walked slowly back to the command vehicle.

CHAPTER 19

The McCarthy twins stood in the back of the half-track. Their combined weight, concentrated in so small a place, canted it at an angle. Luke tried to count how many words they had spoken between them since they'd landed in the Yukon. He stopped at seventeen. That's all there was.

They watched with silent interest as Luke fiddled with the direction finder. Four eyes, barely enough blue for a robin's egg among them, moved in unison. The green splotch on the screen was moving sluggishly, but at least it was moving.

"Okay, here they come," Luke whispered.

"How long?" The McCarthys spoke as one.

"Two hours, tops. I figure they'll pick up speed before long. The main thing was getting them to take the bait. They've done that. Now they'll be anxious to swallow it."

The human bookends grunted, this time in sequence. Luke looked over his shoulder at them, tempted to ask why, then thought better of it. They probably wouldn't know what he was getting at, anyway.

"Ben, what's your read on this?"

"I don't know, Luke. According to Jason Mackenzie, they were pretty heavily armed. He was pretty shook up. He almost blew me away when he sneaked up behind me outside the town. I have to believe they're anxious as hell too. I can't tell if it's exaggeration or not. The Indian guy agrees with Mackenzie. The two of them have combat experience, but it's been a while. I'm just not sure.''

"Tran's satellite photos are inconclusive. Too much cloud cover. I figure that should break before morning. All the feeds from the TIROS satellite show the trailing edge moving our way. We should have about twelve to eighteen hours of clear sky after it breaks. Then it comes down again, hard.''

"We got to finish before then, that's all," Ben said.

"You make it sound easy, Ben.''

"We don't have anything to say about it. We don't get it done then, it doesn't get done at all. What about that other signal, the pulse you picked up on the scanner?''

"I figure that's got to be the payload. It's not a regular beacon. I checked on that. And if you're going to put one on a rocket, you put it on the piece you want to find.''

"How far away is it?''

"Thirty miles.''

"Any chance they missed it?''

"I doubt it. What I can't figure is why they haven't moved in to pick it up before this. They have as much trouble with the clock as we do, maybe more. Something's funny, but I can't piece it together. And I don't know how it fits with the attack on the village. But it has to, somehow.''

"Sabotage?''

"I don't get you, Ben.''

"Well, the thing went off-course. Maybe somebody brought it down on purpose. Maybe whoever did it is just as anxious for it to stay lost as he was for it to get lost in the first place.''

"That sort of thing isn't easy to pull off, especially not in a police state.''

"I disagree. It's probably easier in a police state. If the police are part of it.''

"Why would the KGB or somebody like that want the thing hijacked, especially like this?''

Ben shrugged. "If I knew that, I wouldn't have as many other questions as I do now.''

"Sounds too farfetched to me."

"Maybe. But look, people are looking into sabotage with the *Challenger* and other rockets, those Titans that misfired. If that's worth considering, so is this."

Luke nodded, still unconvinced. "Maybe you're right. But we can't afford to worry about it now. We have a race to win first. And it's probably going to be a demolition derby."

"You don't have to tell me that," Ben said. "I saw what was left of Old Crow, remember? I think we have to assume the worst and take those mothers out as soon as we can. Mr. Nice Guy is only going to get his butt kicked around here."

Luke smiled grimly. "Don't worry about it, Ben. It's been a long time since anybody called me a nice guy."

"To your face, maybe."

The men assembled in the snow. Luke looked at the sky. It seemed lighter. Maybe the break in the weather would arrive ahead of schedule. They were badly outnumbered; they didn't need the odds against them stacked any higher. In fifteen minutes the column was ready to roll. Luke took the lead.

He glanced over his shoulder. The array of sleds behind him looked like nothing so much as a procession of winter toys. He knew the Russians were similarly equipped, but he had the unsettling sensation that he might be leading another children's crusade. He could only hope this one was more successful.

Luke was no stranger to long odds. There was a part of him that reveled in the status of underdog. He was notorious among his friends for taking any bet where the point spread exceeded reason. He never backed the favorite.

SWAT work had been tailor-made for him, at least psychologically. You didn't even get into the game until the bottom of the ninth. And you never had a lead.

He leaned forward to click on the tracking console. The Soviet column glowed dark amber against the gray screen. The patch from the truck was working like a dream. It had been a stroke of genius to hot-wire the truck as a relay station, picking up a feed from Tran and passing it on. The main scanner was plugged into the unit, assigned a backup frequency, and it, too, would play on the road. All he needed

was a plastic sandwich and it would be just like riding the
red-eye.

They had mapped a probable route for the Soviets, based
on the dual givens of the payload location and the logic of
topography. There was a smart route and a quick route. Luke,
giving the Soviets the benefit of the doubt, assumed they had
opted for the quick route. It's what he would have done in
their shoes. And his experience in Vietnam, if it had taught
him anything, had taught him just how unwise it could be to
underestimate your opponent. You could hate him, you could
make fun of him, but by God, you better never think you
were better than he was.

The ass that got kicked could be your own.

They began to roll, and the wind, as if resentful of their
sudden mobility, seemed to redouble. Against the thick gray
overcast, Luke saw a paler, thinner gray, scudding along
ahead of the wind. The snow had thinned too. It still fell, but
for the first time since his arrival, Luke felt as if the swirling
haze came more from the wind than the heavens. That was a
good sign.

But, like always, the blessing was mixed. Watching the
screen, Luke was dismayed to notice the thick amber blob
fragment. The Soviet team had split up. Three separate,
smaller blobs took the place of the single unit. As he watched,
two of the three began to oscillate. At first he was puzzled.
He got Tran on the satellite patch, and the unstumpable
wizard gave him the bad news.

Luke's scanner was picking up the tracking signal from the
main unit, but the other two would only be picked up when in
active radio contact. If they kept radio silence, as they were
likely to do now, they would be invisible. If they could be
provoked to make contact with the main unit, they would
reveal their presence, but that would be intermittent at best,
and you couldn't be expected to provoke what you couldn't
see.

That explained how they had gotten to Old Crow unde-
tected. Watching their monitors, they had concentrated on
only the main unit. Small blips, dismissed as noise or echoes,

had been sporadic traffic between the main unit and the assault team.

Luke dropped off to the side, waiting for Ben's sled to catch up to him. The Apache drew alongside and stopped his own sled. His expression spoke louder than the wind. He knew the news was bad. And all he wanted to know was what he was expected to do about it.

Quickly Luke stretched the situation for the impassive Indian. One of the units had slanted in their direction before dropping off the scope.

"So you want me to go for a sleigh ride in the country and see what I can see, eh, boss?"

"You got it."

"Why is it that the long-knives always use the red man to do their scouting? Haven't you guys learned to read sign yet?"

"Don't knock it. It's just an admission of your inherent superiority . . ."

"Thank you, Great White Father."

". . . in an admittedly inferior capacity, appropriate to your savage state."

"May the coyote gnaw your liver, as long as the rivers shall run and the grass shall grow."

"Look, don't blame me. It was your people who signed the damn treaties. You could have had a lawyer read it over first."

"There were no yuppie Indians. Still aren't."

"There you go, then," Luke said. "It's a small price to pay for such blessed innocence. Take Mackenzie and Silverbird with you. They know the terrain. I want to start chopping away at these guys."

Ben gunned his sled and shot off into the darkness. Luke watched him go, suppressing a shudder of misgiving. When the Apache was out of sight, trailed by Mackenzie and Silverbird, Luke raced past the others to resume his position at the head of the column. To keep his mind off the unpalatable, Luke watched the single, small blip move slowly and inexorably toward the pulsing blob that was its goal.

For a few seconds Luke lost his perspective. The whole

thing was reduced to an absurdly simply video game. All he needed was for some grinning character to bounce out of the periphery to eat the bad guys. He didn't even need the overkill of a pepper shaker or a power pill. It was the ultimate reduction. One on one, his skill against the machine. You could always outwit a static opponent.

For one exhilarating moment it was possible to forget that Ben was out there in the darkness and that he would bleed real blood and break real bones if Luke miscalculated. The others, too, would bleed. Those on both sides. And Luke suddenly remembered why he hated video games. It was the same reason he hated slasher movies, the absurd reduction of the single inevitable human drama . . . death.

Then he had another flash. He was a puppet master without strings. Ben, Mackenzie, and Silverbird were out there alone. Luke had sent them, and Luke was responsible. But if they got in trouble, they were beyond the pale. There was no way for Luke to help them. There wouldn't be time even if, by some slim chance, there was something he could do.

Suddenly, in a way he'd never known, he understood why his commander had never smiled in 'Nam.

War was nothing to smile about.

CHAPTER 20

David Naughton, standing on the tarmac at Eielson Air Force Base just outside of Fairbanks, felt just a little bit foolish. His chin was buried in a fur collar that tickled him unmercifully as he watched the old C-47 being loaded. This was going to be something new for him. He'd been around for twenty years, but this was the first time he'd been anyplace the women didn't go barefoot all year round.

Angola, the Philippines, Guatemala, his Company résumé read like a litany of Third World interventionism. But it was where the action was. He thrived on it. And now he was dressed to the nines in thick fur, like an Eskimo party animal, a stone's throw from the top of the world. It was the place he'd always wanted to be but not in a literal sense.

It was the hurrying that he got off on. Action, no matter how half-baked, was better than sitting around with your nose in intelligence abstracts. Until this morning he hadn't realized how much he missed being on the cutting edge. Movers and shakers didn't waste time reading. That's what college boys were for.

The team was almost ready. The steady rumble of the equipment had stopped. Snow whipped across the runway in small whirls. A team of plows kept after it, worrying it into piles at the edge of the tarmac. The bright yellow plows, blocky and ungainly, whined and snarled. Now and then a blade bit too deeply, scattering sparks behind it.

In fifteen minutes he would be airborne. An hour after that he would be in the catbird seat. He hadn't understood how much it had galled him to sit back and watch others do the fun stuff. Deadly Force was going to get a little surprise. Simpson, he knew, wasn't a bad fellow, but he had just a little too much pride. He wasn't a team player, never had been, or he would have stuck with the Company.

But David Naughton was going to give the rug a pretty good yank. And he'd be there laughing when Simpson landed on his ass. That was all the reason he needed to get this show on the road. He smiled to himself, aware of the cold on his cheeks. He rubbed one hand carelessly over his chin, smearing the protective jelly with his mitten.

There was work to do—and plenty of time to gloat later on. Naughton ran over a mental checklist, fearful that he might have forgotten something. He was a little rusty, he knew. Sitting behind a desk had to dull you a bit, take the edge off finely honed senses. Like anything allowed to fall into disuse, the instincts that kept you alive in the field could fall prey to time.

This was his chance to get it all back. And the fact that it could be the intelligence coup of the decade made it all the more attractive. Stiles Moreland, of course, would get all the credit in the press, assuming anyone ever learned about it. But the insiders, the people whose opinions really counted, would know the truth. It took more than a stuffed shirt to fill the Agency's top slot. And next time David Naughton would be right there at the head of the class. Next time was *his* time.

The team had been assembled on short notice, but Naughton was more than satisfied. Twenty men seemed like a skimpy number, but if things went according to plan, and there was no reason to think they wouldn't, Simpson would carry most of the weight. It was too bad, in a way, to run a number like that on someone who was on the same side, but it was the way the world worked. Getting the prize was more important than how you pulled it off.

Using men drawn from a regular military unit wasn't Naughton's first choice, but time permitted no alternative. At least he had his pick. Working with men from the Army's Arctic Command was better than he could have asked for. Trained at Fort Wainwright, they were used to the kind of conditions they'd be facing. And there was the added advantage of enforceable secrecy.

Hired guns, no matter how hard you tried to keep them quiet, had a tendency to mouth off. The first beer after a mission was usually all the lubricant needed. Half of the mercs Naughton had run were nothing more than neighborhood bullies, anxious to rub somebody's nose in something and, quicker still, to tell anybody who'd listen. With the Polar Bears he wouldn't have to worry about that. A court-martial was all the deterrent one needed.

A man in arctics appeared in the open cargo bay of the C-47. He spotted Naughton and sprinted down the ramp, heading in his direction. Captain Andrew Molson was the officer in charge of the Polar Bear team.

"Mr. Naughton, we're all set."

"All right, Captain. Unless you have any last-minute questions, let's haul ass."

"Actually I do have one question, Mr. Naughton."

"Spit it out."

"Are you sure this insertion will be undetectable?"

"Worried about the odds, Captain?"

"No, sir. But I don't want to count on it if it won't happen. I want my men to know exactly what the score is. It's how I play the game. Rules are rules, and you spooks play by your own set. I understand that, but the lives of my men come first. I remember the Bay of Pigs. Promises have a way of not being kept."

"Look, Molson, if you're too much of a pussy to go along, you can stay here. I already told you, the C-47 is equipped with some experimental gear. It's not a stealth bomber, for chrissake, but it's packing the same electronics. We've been using it to fly munitions into Afghanistan for almost a year.

Nobody's seen us yet. If that's not good enough for you, I'm sorry. Now, if that's all, let's get our asses on the plane.''

"Yes, sir.''

"And Molson . . .''

"Sir?''

"Don't 'sir' me. I'm a civilian.''

Naughton brushed past and walked briskly toward the plane. Molson hesitated a moment, watching him. There was more here than met the eye. Civilian wasn't quite the right description, he thought.

Naughton was a cowboy.

The phone rang, catching Jake O'Bannion in mid-pace. He snatched it from the cradle without breaking stride.

"Yeah, what is it?''

Tran expected the snarl and waited patiently for the chance to say something.''

"Jake, that you?''

"You expected Mayor Koch? What do you want?''

"I got something here I don't like.''

"Why tell *me*?''

"I don't want to alarm Luke unnecessarily. It might be nothing. I just wanted to check something with you.''

The rough veneer vanished in an instant. Jake was all business. "What is it, Tran?''

"Did that guy from Defense, what's his name, the undersecretary, tell you anything about another team going in?''

"In where? Who?''

"I don't know who; I was hoping you did. My last contact with Luke was cut short. But he told me the Soviets had split into three units. He was only able to track one, because the others were maintaining radio silence.''

"So?''

"So, using infrared data and a healthy dose of inferential reasoning, I make five units, not four. Three Soviets and Luke. That's four. Who's the fifth?''

"I don't know, but I sure as hell am going to find out. Tompkins is asleep topside. I think I'll wake him up.''

"You better hurry. I want to know what's going on before I

raise Luke. We're trying to keep the transmissions to a minimum."

"Why?"

"Think about it, man. If we can read them, they can read us. The fewer windows, the fewer opportunities for them to get a fix."

"If they have infrared, and they do, they already know where Luke is. So what's the difference?"

"It's less reliable than radio, more conjectural. Besides, our infrared is better than theirs."

"Yeah, and my old man can beat up your old man."

"What?"

"Nothing, it's an idiom. You damned foreigners never understand. Listen, let me go. I need my energy. Something tells me I'm not going to like what Mr. Tompkins has to say. I'll get back to you as soon as I can."

Jake steamrollered to the doorway, pressed the electronic lock, and hollered.

"Watson, come here. I want you."

The unlucky Watson, his eyes bulging, his chin nestled in his neck to protect his jugular, sprinted down the hallway. "What is it, Mr. O'Bannion?"

"You stay here and keep an eye on things. I'm going topside for a few minutes. Anything happens, and I mean anything, you get me on the horn. You got that?"

"Yes, sir."

And Jake was gone. He moved quickly for a big man. His feet slapped the concrete floor like the clapping of a circus seal. At the elevator he pressed the call button, then turned his back on the door to wait. He felt about elevators the way other New Yorkers did about cops. They were never there when you needed one.

A pneumatic hiss signaled the car's arrival, and Jake backed in without looking. God help anyone in his way. He took the car to the aboveground complex, bouncing nervously on the balls of his feet, as if to hurry the car along. When the door finally opened, he was already on the move. Careening down the hallway, he nearly flattened a young woman, also hurrying along, her nose buried in some computer printout.

"Heads up," Jake said, snarling as he sidestepped her on the run. By the time she looked up, Jake was long gone.

He carried a flat plastic card in one hand, extending it as he neared the control door separating the business area from the living quarters. He slipped the card into the electronic lock, then punched in the day's code. Without the card and the number, you couldn't get from one section of the complex to the other.

He drummed his fingers on the keypad. When the heavy steel door slid back noiselessly, he stepped through. The door closed automatically. It was a risky portal. Programmed automatically to close in five seconds, unless otherwise instructed by a card-carrying employee of Deadly Force, Inc., it lacked a safety stop. You got through in the allotted time or left a piece of yourself behind.

Steaming at full throttle toward Tompkins's room, Jake began to mumble to himself. The closer he got, the louder he mumbled. By the time he reached the door, the mumble had become a low rumble, like a thunderstorm just over the horizon. He didn't bother to knock.

Awakened by the racket, the Undersecretary of State sat up in bed. He clicked on the reading lamp on a nightstand and reached for his glasses. "What's going on?" He croaked the words out through sleep-stiffened lips.

"Who else did you send in besides Luke? And don't try to bullshit me, Tompkins. I want to know, and I mean right now."

"Send where? What are you talking about?"

"There's another team up there, isn't there?"

"No, of course not. If we were going to send someone else, we wouldn't have needed Mr. Simpson, now would we?" Tompkins, pleased with his logic, sat back on the pillow.

"You're lying to me."

"Of course I'm not lying. Why would I do that?"

"Because it's what you do for a living. All you federal assholes are paid for it. It's a prerequisite for the job."

"Why don't you calm down and tell me what's happened?"

"I'll tell you what's happened. Tran has spotted another team, besides the three Russian units. That's what happened."

"It's not ours. It can't be." Tompkins sat bolt upright. Jake figured either he didn't know or he was a better actor than his boss ever was. "I mean, I'm sure I would have been informed if there had been another insertion. But even so, it can only be backup. What other reason could there be?"

"What good's backup if you don't know it's there?"

"I don't follow you."

Not bothering to conceal his exasperation, Jake said, "If Luke doesn't know these guys are there, he can't ask them for help, can he?"

"And he doesn't know?"

"Not yet. Tran just spotted them. I thought we'd try to find out what you knew about it, before we contacted him. If you don't know about it, you damn well better get on the phone and find out."

Tompkins sat up, dangling his feet over the side of the bed. "All right, give me a minute to wake up."

"You don't need it." Jake walked to the side of the bed and grabbed the telephone. He shoved it roughly into Tompkins's chest. Even the crack of plastic on bone didn't slow him down. "You know how this thing works. Use it!"

"Mr. O'Bannion, look, I know you're concerned, but I have my own orders. I'll make the call, but you'll have to leave me alone. I won't make the call unless you do."

"How do I know you'll tell the truth?"

"You won't. Whether you stay here or not. What have you got to lose?"

Jake grumbled to himself but nodded. "I'll be right outside. Make it snappy."

CHAPTER 21

"I put them right about here, Luke." Ben Sanchez stabbed at the map with his finger. "About five miles away."

"How many?"

"I'd guess twenty-five to thirty. Two armored personnel carriers. They can handle six to eight men. Plus six motor-sleds. They're the two-man variety, but we didn't get close enough to tell whether they were fully loaded."

Luke turned to one of the Canadians. "Jason, you know the area. Anything special about it? Anything that might give us an advantage?"

"You don't have a nuke, I guess." Mackenzie laughed uneasily.

"Let's just hope *they* don't. They have tactical nukes, artillery, just like we do. Ben, you see anything along the lines of artillery?"

"No, the APCs were just that. Cannons. Probably heavy machine guns mounted somewhere, but I think they were primarily recon units."

"Look," Mackenzie said, "see this point here, where the Bluefish cuts back? There's a notch there, high ground on both sides. They're going to want to cut through there to save time. The terrain is too hilly for the APCs, except along the river."

"Is there any way around it?" Luke asked. He glanced at the monitor off to his right. The steadily pulsing blip of the payload seemed to keep time with his heart rate. "Remember, here's where they want to go." Luke indicated a small penciled circle on the map. "If Tran's right, that's where the payload is. And he has to be. There's no other explanation for that signal."

"No, no way around. None that makes sense, anyhow. They'd add twenty miles to the trip, at least. And none of it easy."

"Then it looks like the notch is what we want."

"You got to keep in mind that the sleds can maneuver okay in here, though. It's just the APCs that would have trouble. Any chance they'll split up and send the sleds overland, the most direct route?"

"Who knows?" Luke held his hands out, palms up. "I wish to Christ I knew."

"Would you do it?" Mackenzie asked.

"Hell, no. Not in a box this tight. I'm not that stupid."

"Let's hope they're not, either," Ben said.

"What about the others?" Rick Silverbird had spoken for the first time. "Where are they?"

"We're not sure, Rick," Luke answered. "All we know for sure is what we see with our own eyes and what Tran can pick up for us. The main hot spot, radiowise, is back this way. But that only has to be one vehicle, maybe with a small detachment to defend it. There could be three or four separate teams out in the field. None of them would be too large. I don't know which would be better: three fairly sizable units that outnumber us three to one, or a bunch of smaller ones we have to chase around like balls of mercury on the floor."

"Why don't we just take this one out and worry later?"

"You got it." Luke folded the map and stuffed it into his pocket. He looked at the men gathered around him. Counting himself, they numbered ten. If you assumed Conroy was virtually worthless, which Luke did, it was nine. Three to one wasn't very good odds, but you had to play the hand you were dealt.

"Conroy, you stay in the APC with Calvin and Roland."

"I can take care of myself, Simpson."

"Maybe, but I want you where somebody can keep an eye on you. Besides, Calvin likes baby-sitting."

Steeples grunted.

Luke stepped out of the tent, letting the canvas slap to behind him. The others followed him out into the cold. The sky above was clear, but the air felt raw. Tran's window was going to close in a couple of hours. Luke already felt like a blind man in a house of mirrors. Everyplace he groped, he felt the same cold, featureless surface. He took a long breath and walked to his sled.

He clicked on the monitor, picking up the feed from the main unit in the tent. He watched the blips, then made the decision he had wanted to avoid. Grabbing the mike, he called Calvin in the APC.

"Calvin, I think we better go without the feed."

"Luke, you sure?"

"We're in a bind, buddy. I'd rather go blind and let them try to guess where we are."

"That's a deep hole to fall in, Luke."

"You got a better idea, I'd love to hear it."

Steeples laughed. Luke watched the screen. He smiled when the number of blips went down to two. Now they had only the main Soviet unit and the rocket payload on the screen—and a handful of invisible pawns on a white chessboard.

Luke strapped himself into the bucket seat of his sled. He turned to watch the others do the same. When everybody was strapped in, he cranked up the sled. The soft *thrum* of the small engines was suddenly drowned by the guttural roar of the APC. The big APC diesel settled down to a steady grumble, and Luke released the brake.

He listened to the swish of his runners on the crisp snow. The dull pulse of the engine rumbled through the floorboard. Luke visualized an equilateral triangle in his mind. Five miles away a Soviet detachment was racing toward the same insignificant notch in the same godforsaken wasteland he was. And they each had five miles to cover. He only hoped the race went to the swift. And victory to the just.

The terrain was rough, rolling tundra, the snow so deeply
drifted that most irregularities had been reduced to gentle
swells. Here and there a hardy shrub broke through the crust,
its twisted branches a grotesque tangle of darkness against the
brilliant white. The shadows looked blue in the darkness.

Ahead, the land rose gradually. In the far distance, beyond
the range of sight, it rose more sharply, peaking at the bank
of the Bluefish River. The water, if it flowed at all, would be
under thick ice. Luke realized it made an ideal highway for
the heavy Soviet vehicles. In the short run, it gave them an
advantage.

Behind him, Luke heard the steady drum of the other
vehicles. The small engines whined like angry insects, the
sound sharp-edged in the cold air. He peered back over his
shoulder, counting shadows in the dark.

Jake O'Bannion paced impatiently. What was taking Tompkins so damned long? The man had been on the phone for
twenty minutes. The dull rumble of his voice drifted through
the door, but Jake could understand nothing of what was
being said. Once or twice the sound was sharp, as if Tompkins were arguing with someone.

That didn't sound like good news to Jake.

He jerked a pack of Marlboros out of his pocket, losing his
grip in anger. The red-and-white box pinwheeled through the
air, spilling its contents as it spun. Jake angrily hurled his
lighter after the package. The cheap plastic cracked on the
hardwood floor, sending splinters and a small metal wheel
skidding along the wall.

Jake puffed as he bent to retrieve a cigarette. Still bent
over, he fished a half-empty book of matches out of his shirt
pocket. The gritty strip of the striking surface was almost
rubbed away. Jake struck it sharply, nearly tearing the head
from the match. It caught in a sudden burst, burning his
thumb. He cursed, lit the cigarette, then squeezed the flame
out between thumb and forefinger.

Jake took a quick drag, then scrambled after the other
cigarettes. As his fingers closed around the last one, he heard
Tompkins open his door. Jake got to his feet as the undersecretary stepped into the hall.

"Well, what did you find out?"

"You're not going to like what I have to say."

"Tell me about it," Jake snapped.

The sky was turning dark gray. Luke checked his watch. It was nearly sunrise. The light would flood the sky in another twenty minutes. He felt absently for the tinted googles dangling around his neck. Ahead, a darker gray, like a thick line, bulked across the horizon. Beyond it, he knew, was the Bluefish River. And what else? he wondered.

Luke held up his left hand. He popped the clutch on the sled and coasted to a halt. Ben slid up alongside him, their sleds nearly touching.

"You wait here. I'm going to take a look around," Luke said. "Tell Calvin to kill his engine. That damn thing sounds like a locomotive. Their own engines will cover it if they're moving, but if they beat us here, they'll hear us for sure."

"I think we should push on. We can leave the APC here, but we're cutting it too close. You can't get there and back in time for us all to make it to the cutoff, and you can't radio for us to follow. And if they get past us, it's down to a footrace. I don't like the odds in that case."

"You're right. But I don't want the APC. Tell Calvin to wait here."

"Right." Ben kicked his sled into a tight circle and skidded back toward the armored behemoth chugging impatiently at the tail end of the line. A moment later he was back.

Luke slid into a sprint, the others hard on his tail. The sun was almost up now. The sky was a yellowish gray, shading into a hard, blue-white glare. Luke had expected a fuller, redder sunrise, but an overcast on the horizon signaled heavy weather and cut down on the fireworks.

Luke yanked his goggles into place with his left hand, keeping a tight rudder as he bounced over the hard crust of snow. The runners hissed constantly as he pushed his sled to its maximum speed. Behind him, the chugging sleds added their own voices to the chorus. The ridge line was just a thousand yards ahead.

Again Luke held up his hand. He killed his engine and

unbelted while the others watched. Kicking his boots into snowshoes, he trudged a hundred yards ahead. Straining his ears, he pulled the tight hood of his parka aside. The dull throb of his own contingent was the only unnatural sound he could hear. He peered through the glare toward the ridge line, looking for anything that might give him a clue, a puff of smoke, a startled bird, an unexpected flash of light glancing off glass or polished steel.

Luke felt strange, standing in the wilderness. For a man who made his living by relying on modern science and often had saved his own life by the skin of his high-tech teeth, searching the sky like an aboriginal wanderer was too anomalous for comfort.

He looked back at the small force he commanded, each loaded down with as much death as he could carry, and felt the obscene absurdity of it. The pristine beauty of the frozen wilderness, as white as the very idea of innocence, was about to be defiled by high explosives and the acrid smoke of politics in action. Luke cleared his throat and spat into the snow, trying to rid his mouth of a bitter taste.

He plodded back toward the empty sled. He got in without a word. Ben sat alongside, watching him silently. Luke kicked his engine over and slammed it into gear.

Ben leaned in, cupping his hands to funnel his words. "I know exactly how you feel, Luke."

Luke sighed. He reached out to clap Ben on the shoulder and popped the clutch. His sled lurched ahead, throwing him back against the seat. He veered off to the right, steering for the highest of several hills in the small cluster that marked the river's course.

Hitting the upgrade at a flat-out run, he skidded over the bumpy rise, killing his engine as he neared the ridge line. The sled coasted a few yards, then came to a halt. He jumped from the sled and sprinted to the crest of the hill. Dropping to his stomach, he fought the blinding glare to stare upstream. There was no sign of the Soviet unit.

Luke hauled a pair of binoculars from the deep pockets of his parka, looping their cord around his neck. He scanned the flat plane of the river's snowy crust. It was unbroken. No one had passed by since the last snow had fallen. The sun was low in the sky, but its light was a brilliant fuzz, blurred across the sky from end to end. Even behind the goggles it hurt his eyes.

Ben dropped to the snow beside him. Mackenzie was with him. "Think we ought to put somebody on the other bank?" Ben asked.

"I don't know if we can risk it, Ben. They're liable to be here any minute."

"I think we should try it," Mackenzie said. "Those guys mean business. Any edge we got, we better use it."

"He's right, Luke," Ben said. "I'll take Rick and Jason across. It'll only take five minutes."

"Okay, but hurry. And take a half dozen LAW rockets with you. Those APCs may not be packing artillery, but they can take a lot of firepower without a scratch. We'll have some on this side too. I want to take them out first. When they show, let the APCs get clear before you cut loose."

"Got it."

Luke watched them sprint downhill. Ben already had the LAW rockets on his sled. He filled Silverbird in on the plan, and Mackenzie dropped onto Rick's sled, leaving his own behind. The two sleds pulled out of line, Ben's in the lead. Instead of coming straight up the hill, Ben wisely cut an angle toward a gap between it and the next. He kept the hill between himself and the upstream site. The sleds picked up speed, heading down toward the water.

The river was only a hundred yards across, and the crossing took less than a minute. Luke held his breath as the sleds climbed the shallow bank on the opposite side, then slipped between two low hills and disappeared.

A moment later he heard a rumble to the right. Canting his glasses in that direction, he caught sight of a thin wisp of black smoke dissipating in the light breeze. It was little more than a slight smudge against the glare.

A heavy metal bulk broke into the clear, its treads churning the snow along the near bank of the river. Several sleds trailed along behind, goslings struggling to keep near the goose. Luke counted the swarm of smaller vehicles, six in all.

A second APC brought up the rear, lagging somewhat behind, whether to spread the weight on the ice or for some other reason that Luke couldn't guess.

He brought the glasses to bear on the opposite hill. There was no sign of Ben and the others. "Patrick, bring me one of the LAWs. Make it snappy."

The larger of the McCarthy brothers waddled up the slope, a pair of LAWs in one hand. He tossed one to Luke, who caught it one-handed, and hit the snow a few yards to Luke's left. The armor-piercing rockets packed a hell of a punch. One should be enough to take out an APC.

"Which one do you want, Luke?" Patrick asked, aiming at the rear APC.

Still scanning the far side of the river for Ben, Luke didn't answer right away. He dropped the glasses and hefted the LAW to his shoulder. "I'll take the lead car."

"You got it."

"Fire on three. Ready . . . one . . . two . . . three . . ."

The rockets whooshed off almost simultaneously. Luke buried his face in the snow. Patrick let out a whoop, and a second later Luke heard the awesome detonation as one rocket found its mark.

Luke watched through the glasses as the lead APC swelled, then burst into a smoky ball, tinged with orange. Like some weird, ugly flower, it seemed to grow before his eyes. He switched to the rear vehicle and saw a gaping hole in the armor plate, just to the rear of the main hatch. Patrick had been right on the money, but the hit was far from fatal. Luke imagined the swirling cloud of razor-sharp shrapnel inside the APC and shuddered.

A moment later a small flash on the opposite hill announced Ben's LAW. A high-pitched whine screamed across the frozen air, and a thin skein of smoke pointed an accusing finger at the launch point. The rocket slammed home, and the APC, belching smoke and flame out of the hole Patrick had ripped in its near side, crumpled like a ball of tinfoil. The air filled with a horrendous creak, like the sound of sheet metal tearing, and one end of the ruined vehicle shot straight up. The other sank out of sight.

The twin blasts had shattered the ice beneath it. A second later there was nothing left but a boiling black hole in the thick ice. Small clouds of smoke rose to the surface in bubbles and drifted off like minor storms as the diesel fuel continued to burn inside the ruptured vehicle.

Like angry bees defending the hive, the sleds buzzed up the slode toward Ben's position. Ben appeared briefly, then vanished. The plume of smoke left by his second LAW ripped sidewise and tangled as the rocket slammed into the lead sled.

The blast took out two of the six sleds. The remaining four spun in circles, uncertain where to go. As if their drivers had suddenly realized their vulnerability, they turned and headed toward the bank, just below Luke's position.

A cry ripped through the air, and a moment later Ben's sled crested the rise. It seemed to hang in midair for a second, then tipped its nose forward and veered to one side, skidding down the slope.

The four Russian sleds, two mounted with light machine guns, charged up the snowy slope in front of Luke. So far they didn't seem to realize what waited for them at the crest of the hill.

Luke brought his Suomi down, snicked off the safety, and held his breath. Beside him, Patrick McCarthy pulled the pin on a concussion grenade, pushing his own Suomi to one side.

As Luke watched, Patrick's arm moved in a graceful arc. The grenade spun away out of sight. A loud blast signaled that it was time to move. Luke shot to his feet, the Suomi in his right hand. Together he and Patrick charged over the ridge.

Luke began firing as soon as he cleared the hilltop. Below, two sleds still sped toward him. He noticed one on its side, its driver motionless beside it. He swept the Finnish SMG in a broad arc, aiming low to compensate for the kick of the weapon.

The lead sled sped straight into the hail of fire. The second, bearing two men, was a little slower. Its machine gun opened up, and Luke dived to the ground.

Patrick, oblivious to the fire, rolled downhill, his arms in tight to his body. The sled sped past him, and he spread his legs to arrest his descent. He was struggling to his feet as the sled spun into a tight 180.

Patrick swung the Suomi up and cut loose. The hammering of the weapon drowned the snarl of the sled's engine. The gunner slumped forward over his .30-caliber, and Patrick tossed a tight coil of slugs at the driver.

Caught in the chest, the driver lost control of the sled. He slumped over the controls, throwing the sled into a continuous circle. Patrick struggled across the snow, trying to keep his balance.

A snarl to the left caught Luke's ear. He turned just as the remaining Russian sled broke into the open. It, too, was mounted with a machine gun. The gunner opened up, catching Patrick by surprise. He dived to his left as Ben roared up the bank.

Ben's sled was faster, and cut at an angle across the slope. Luke emptied his magazine, keeping the Russian gunner off-balance. Ben drew closer, leapt from his sled, and fell prone on the snow. He brought his Suomi up and stitched the driver across the chest. Small dark blots spattered the front of the driver's parka.

The machine gunner swung his weapon in Ben's direction. He was a hair too slow. Ben drilled him with the last few rounds in his magazine. He fell backward off the sled, which tipped to its side and slid slowly downhill.

That quickly it was over.

End of round one.

Now all they had to do was count their scars and figure what the next step should be.

CHAPTER 22

David Naughton stared out the window of the C-47. The bright glare hurt his eyes, but he refused to turn away. He squinted against the light, as if he were accumulating grace for his suffering. In less than an hour he and his team would touch down outside the village of Old Crow. It was thirty miles from the source of the radio pulse NSA had picked up; any closer might spook the Soviet search team or tip his hand to Luke Simpson. Neither prospect was one that appealed to him.

He ran alternate scenarios in his head, projecting them against the glaring disk of the C-47 window. Like overexposed film, they offered more outline than detail. Despite his bravado with Stiles Moreland, he had reservations about just how easy it might be to pull off his masterstroke.

He watched Andrew Molson, sitting sidesaddle two seats in front of him. Molson seemed to have an easy rapport with his men, and Naughton envied him. He regretted his own brusqueness with the captain just before takeoff. He knew now that it was stage fright, the need to reassert his control, not only over the circumstances of the mission but also over himself. He had been out of circulation too long. Watching the bleak landscape slip by under the wing, he wondered whether it might not, after all, be a game for men younger than himself. With an impatient sweep of his arm he brushed the thought away like a physical thing.

Hauling himself to his feet, Naughton walked toward the front of the plane. The seat next to Molson was empty. He dropped into it with a grunt. "The old bones ain't what they used to be, Captain," he mumbled.

Molson ignored him. He continued to talk to the young man seated across the aisle. The small passenger cabin was roughly outfitted. Most of the plane's fuselage was given over to the transport of matériel. Naughton felt cramped. Molson ignoring him made the space seem even more confined.

He stared at the captain's back, and at the blurred edge of the Polar Bear insignia on his sleeve. He wanted to apologize for his earlier behavior but didn't know how. Making amends wasn't his long suit. He wasn't even sure it was in the deck he played with.

Molson clapped his hands and stood up, as if his conversation had come to a close. He turned to look at Naughton. "You okay, Mr. Naughton?"

"Yeah, why?"

"You look a little green around the gills."

"Been a while since I've been in combat."

"I thought this was a recovery mission."

"It is, of a sort."

"What do you mean, 'of a sort'? Is it or isn't it? I told you, I didn't want any surprises. What the hell are you trying to pull?"

In spite of his resolve, Naughton bristled. "I'm not trying to pull anything. And you'd do well to remember that I am in charge here."

"Maybe so, but you damn well better tell me what's going on."

"Or what?"

"Or you'll go out in the fucking snow by yourself."

"Are you telling me you'll disobey my orders?"

"What do you think? Read my lips, Naughton."

"All right, all right, let's slow down."

"Then tell me what the hell is going on."

Naughton stood up. He walked toward the rear of the plane, motioning for Molson to follow him. The other members of the unit affected disinterest.

Fifteen minutes later a shaken Molson resumed his seat. Naughton stayed behind. In briefing the young captain, the enormity of the risk they were taking came home to him for the first time. He walked over to the last window in the passenger cabin. The glare outside seemed darker. He wondered whether it was a change in the light or in his perspective. And if it mattered.

Tran Cao stared at his telemetry monitor in bafflement. The latest radio picture, his sharpest yet, thanks to the welcome blessing of clear sight and good weather, seemed to contradict his expectations.

He rummaged through the pile of computer printouts and digital photo analogs on his desk. He could have sworn there was one fewer hot spot on his previous analysis. The infrared dump from Big Bird had come in a half hour before. Crash processing had yielded the latest images in the Old Crow vicinity. But there was more there than met the eye, or at least more than had met it the last time around.

One of the hot spots had faded considerably. That would be the ruins of the town itself. The embers, despite the cold, would radiate for several more hours. It wasn't possible to hide that kind of ambient heat, not even in the Arctic.

He sketched the locations with a grease pencil on a transparency, then slid it into place over his previous chart. Sure enough, there was a new one. And it wasn't as simple as something having changed locations. All his previous data supported the current location of every heat source but one. Photoverification was not going to be possible for several hours. He'd have to get his hunch to NSA and hope they would agree to turn the Big Bird's cameras on his coordinates. By then, whatever it was might well have moved. Even with a crash priority the next photo pass wasn't for more than two hours. By then, it might be too late.

His first thought was a second Soviet insertion, but it didn't make sense. Why wait so long? Or had the first team run into some trouble and asked for assistance? It would take forty-eight hours to analyze the traffic, and even then, he'd have to have some idea what he was looking for. The sheer volume of intercepted transmissions was too great. Tran began pacing in his frustration. He stared at the data, walked a tight circle around the table, and came right back to the same point. When he got there, nothing had changed.

And why the hell hadn't he heard from Jake? The damn Irishman was probably too busy chewing somebody out to tend to business. As soon as he thought it, he regretted it. O'Bannion worked as hard as anyone else. But he was so damn irascible, sometimes he got wrapped up in how angry he was and forgot to pay attention to details.

Tran reached for the phone. He listened to it ring impatiently. After what seemed like an hour, O'Bannion finally got on the line. He didn't sound happy.

"Tran, I was just going to call you. We got problems."

"What kind of problems?"

"You were right, there was another unit sent in."

"Russian?"

"No, one of ours."

"Oh. For a minute, there, you had me worried."

"You still should be."

"What's going on?"

"You sure you want to know?"

Calvin Steeples stared at the radar screen in front of him. In the darkness of the APC, the green glow was harsh. It tinted everything with a sickly cast. He looked over his shoulder at Malcom Conroy, who slumped in a seat as if oblivious to his surroundings. The steady sweep of the radar was making Steeples dizzy. The monotonous beep each time it completed a 360-degree sweep was beginning to irritate him. Using the radar was a calculated risk. No one was sure how sophisticated the Russians were at detecting defensive radar. But the last thing Deadly Force needed was to sit there with its eyes closed.

Calvin flipped the sound switch and leaned back. At least now he wouldn't have to listen to it. Watching the sweep with half an eye, he busied himself with some safety checks. The APC had been sluggish, and something told him they were a long way from out of the woods. In a pinch, this big baby would have to perform. There were no second chances.

The small blur almost escaped notice. Calvin blinked once, then looked again. It was still there, the pale, rapidly fading blip just inside the sweep perimeter. He checked his settings.

The sweep was set for a twenty-five-mile radius. He switched to the fifty-mile setting, and the blip darted toward the center of the screen. For a second he hoped it was some glitch, an echo of some kind. But the sweep came around, and there it was again. He watched it move steadily away to the southwest.

What puzzled him was why he hadn't seen it before. Based on its current course, it would have flown nearly overhead. But he would have seen it on the scope a long time ago. He checked his maps and fixed the bogie at a point just west of Old Crow. It had been close to the perimeter, so it was possible he had caught some bush pilot making a circle over Old Crow, maybe drawn by the absence of contact with its residents for a couple of days. But that hypothesis didn't fly, either. Whatever it was, it was too damn big to be a two-seater.

His first instinct was to wake Conroy, but something told him not to. He looked at the sleeping CIA man as if he sensed some hidden connection between the sleeper and the sighting. But there was no way Conroy had been able to contact anyone. He hadn't let the kid out of his sight for two days. That left one explanation. Whatever it was, it was leaving. That had to mean that either it had been there at Old Crow all along or it had somehow managed to sneak in unnoticed.

Calvin ran a quick check in his head. Based on the size of the blip, he guessed it had to be a four-engine plane—a cargo job or an airliner. And for it to appear so suddenly, either it had just taken off or it had suddenly lost some sort of electronic concealment. If they just got company, it was unexpected, the worst kind.

He debated whether to raise Luke on the radio. Breaking silence was a risk. The question was: Was it riskier than not breaking it? The answer depended on what had just taken place back at the ruined village. Calvin didn't even want to think about the possibilities. He glanced at Conroy again. The kid was sound asleep.

Calvin pulled his parka around him and slipped up through the hatch. He let the heavy metal plate down gingerly, letting it seat without a sound. The two remaining sleds were tethered to the rear of the APC. Calvin untied one sled, struggling in the deep snow. He towed it off into the drifts. At fifty yards he climbed on and turned the ignition. The small engine sputtered loudly, like a reluctant lawn mower on the first day of spring. Smoke belched from the exhaust for a few seconds, at first black, then gray. Finally it turned a wispy white, not much more substantial than steam.

Steeples engaged the clutch and felt the sled lurch beneath him. Far ahead he could see smoke rising in thick black gouts. He gunned the sled's engine and roared downhill, picking up speed. The sled handled easily, sliding quickly through turns and bouncing with rough effortlessness over the larger bumps in the snow.

As he drew closer to the columns of smoke, now beginning to thin a bit, he pulled his hood loose a bit to listen. Over the pounding of the engine he could hear small-arms fire. He let go of the hood and gave the sled full throttle. The little engine labored into the upgrade, and the sound of gunfire suddenly died.

Nearing the crest of the hill, Calvin slowed the engine, dropping back to a crawl. He gave the engine just enough gas to keep from sliding backward down the hill. Listening closely, he heard voices. He shut the engine down and rolled off into the snow, reaching back for a pair of snowshoes. He struggled getting the heavy boots into the clamps but finally managed to snug them down over heel and toe.

Getting to his feet uncertainly, he bent to grab a Valmet 7.62-mm assault rifle from its sheath behind the bucket seat. Like the Suomi, it was of Finnish design. And who better than the Finns to build a gun for Arctic adventures? They had held off the entire Red Army for a year at the beginning of World War II. Without the Suomi, it would have been over a lot sooner.

Calvin flapped his ungainly way up the hill, stopping just below the crest. The sky was thickening, the light beginning to fade, as if it were a liquid leaching away into the ground. It looked like snow.

Again.

At the ridge line Calvin flopped forward onto his stomach and wriggled forward until he could see over it. At the foot of the hill several small figures in white parkas struggled with the prostrate forms of others identically attired. The river ice beyond was littered with wreckage, as was the slope ahead of him. Several sleds, most shattered to useless junk, lay on their sides.

Calvin smiled when he realized the black hole in the ice had swallowed an APC. Things couldn't have gone all that badly if they had taken both out. One of the figures at the bottom of the hill looked up, letting go of the feet it had been holding. The man reached for his rifle, and Calvin ducked down as another knocked the rifle away.

The man waved, then jumped on a sled. He gunned the engine and charged straight toward him. Calvin snicked the Valmet's safety off. He sighted down the hill, allowing for the steep decline. His finger was quivering on the trigger before he realized the charging man was Luke.

The sled spun sideways, throwing a sharp, stinging spray of snow into his face.

Luke grinned. "What brings you out this way?"

"We got some company."

The grin disappeared.

CHAPTER 23

"Colonel Borlov, I think you should look at this." Schevardnadze rolled his chair to one side, making room for his commanding officer. He pointed at the screen. "Here, this."

"What is it?"

"I don't know. It just appeared."

"What do you mean, 'appeared'? From where?"

"From nowhere. Right there in the middle of the screen."

"What location?"

"As near as I can tell, just outside the village you destroyed."

"That's ridiculous. It's not possible. Captain Chertok, look at this, please. Give me your interpretation."

Chertok leaned in to peer at the screen. "I'm afraid I can't be of much help to you, Colonel. Electronics is not something I know much about. It is Major Schevardnadze's province."

"And I already know what the major thinks. He claims he doesn't know what it is. But I don't believe he'd tell me what this was, even if he knew."

Borlov stared at the screen as if he could compel it to explain itself.

"I—" Schevardnadze, about to defend himself, stopped. A

loud crackle echoed through the interior of the communications vehicle.

"What was that?" Borlov demanded.

"Ermine Leader . . . Ermine Leader . . . do you read me? Ermine Leader, this is Ermine Two. Come in."

"That's Lieutenant Ekizian," Schevardnadze shouted.

"Get out of my way, Major." Borlov pushed his way to the console, shoving Schevardnadze roughly to one side. He grabbed the hand mike and fumbled with the switch. "Ermine Two, this is Ermine Leader. What's happening out there?"

The speaker crackled with an ear-piercing intensity, obscuring the transmission. Borlov shouted into his mike, "Repeat, Ermine Two, repeat. Your transmission is breaking up. Repeat."

Schevardnadze pushed Borlov to one side and yanked the mike free. "Lieutenant Ekizian, is that you? This is Major Schevardnadze. What is going on?"

"We were attacked. I don't know who . . . they . . . the . . . everybody's dead . . ."

"Where are you?"

"I'm not sure . . . I . . . when the attack began, we were on the Bluefish. . . ."

"Ask him how many of them there were," Borlov said.

"Lieutenant, how many in the attack force?"

"I don't know. It all happened so fast. They destroyed MT-LBs right away. They were on both sides of the river. Rockets . . . they used some kind of rockets."

"So it wasn't locals," Chertok mumbled. "They don't have that kind of hardware."

"Are you all right? Have you been wounded?"

"Yes, sir, but it's minor. I'll be okay. The bleeding has stopped."

"Stay where you are, Lieutenant. Hold your mike open. I'll try to get a fix."

Schevardnadze clicked on the scanner. Three blips appeared on the screen. The large pulsing blob of the payload was immediately obvious. Ekizian could have been either of the other two. "All right, Lieutenant, click your mike on and off three times." He stared hard at the two remaining blips. After a few seconds one blinked three times in rapid succession.

"Okay, got it. You stay right where you are. We'll be there as soon as we can. Now close your mike and maintain radio silence. If I spotted you, somebody else can do it too."

Borlov spread his arms backward, stretching them like a young bird trying his wings. "Very impressive, Major. Very impressive, indeed. Perhaps you are a military man, after all."

Schevardnadze said nothing.

Borlov continued. "It's too bad we won't be able to deliver on your promise."

"What do you mean?" Schevardnadze turned abruptly to stare at Borlov. "Why not?"

"Think about it, Major. Use your head. It could be a trap."

"But that was Lieutenant Ekizian. How could it be a trap?"

"You said it yourself, Major. You found him. Do you think that possibility escapes the opposition, whoever they are? Why wouldn't they just sit there and wait for us? They already ambushed Ermine Two. It would be a simple matter to do it again."

"But we can't leave him out there."

"Of course we can. In fact, we have no choice, Major. If you think about it clearly, you'll understand that. We have no choice. Our first priority is the recovery. Lieutenant Ekizian is a soldier, he knows that. We'll pick him up after we recover the payload. If there's time."

"But—"

"That's it, Major. End of discussion."

"At least let me tell him we're not coming. You can't just leave him out there, expecting us."

"On the contrary, Major. If I am right and it is a setup, it is better if he expects us. Because if he is, they are. And while they wait, we will be attaining our primary objective. You have unwittingly countered a very clever scheme."

Schevardnadze looked at Borlov. His jaw quivered as if he

wanted to say something. Then he turned and stalked out of the half-track. He left the door open.

"Try to talk some sense into him, Captain," Borlov said. "But don't try too hard. Major Schevardnadze has rather limited utility."

Chertok nodded. He followed Schevardnadze out into the snow. He spotted the major several meters away, sitting on a mound of snow. Chertok walked quietly, wondering what he would say. Schevardnadze seemed not to notice him. Chertok dropped down beside the major. He said nothing.

Schevardnadze turned to see who had joined him. When he realized it was Chertok, he turned away. "I suppose you agree with him, and he's sent you out here to convince me."

"Yes."

"On both counts?"

"Yes, on both counts."

"Well, don't waste your time."

"Major, there is nothing you can do for Lieutenant Ekizian. As Colonel Borlov said, if we get lucky and recover the payload quickly, we might be able to pick him up on the way to the rendezvous. If not, if it takes us too long, well . . ."

"You're as bad as he is, but I guess that doesn't surprise me. I know what you are. I know all about you."

"Don't be too certain of that, Major."

Schevardnadze made no sign that Chertok's words meant anything to him. He might not even have heard.

The captain continued. "If you really want to help the lieutenant, then I suggest you get us to our destination as quickly as you can."

"Whatever you say, Captain." He stood and walked slowly back to the command unit. Chertok followed at a discreet distance. When he stepped into the half-track, Borlov was all business. It was as if the previous exchange had never taken place.

"Major, is there anything you can do to help us locate the force that attacked Ermine Two?"

Grateful for the apparent amnesty, Schevardnadze answered immediately. "I don't know, Colonel. They don't show on the scanner. If we can get them to break radio silence, maybe. But I don't know how we can go about that."

"Suppose we contact them directly," Chertok suggested.

"And how do we do that?" Borlov asked.

"We don't know what happened to Corporal Karpov. Or to his handset. Let's suppose, for the sake of argument, that they have it. Suppose they captured him and have been monitoring our communications, even as sporadic as they have been. Couldn't we use that to our advantage?"

Borlov brushed the suggestion aside. "Not likely, Captain."

"No, Captain Chertok is right. They *have* been doing just that."

"What makes you so sure?" Borlov snapped.

"I thought I heard something before, when the truck was damaged. I couldn't get a clear signal. Then, when the equipment was down, I thought it must have been a mistake. Later, when I tried again, I caught the tail end of something. I thought it might be Karpov, but . . ."

"And you never told me, Major? Why not?"

"There wasn't anything to tell. Nothing conclusive. I didn't think it—"

"You didn't think. Period. I should have—"

"Colonel, let's get down to business," Chertok said, cutting in. "Major, what can we do to take advantage of the possibility?"

"Well, if they are monitoring us, I suppose we can send them false communications, let them act on that basis. We can manipulate them, I suppose."

Borlov stroked his chin. He seemed to be mulling over the idea. "There are risks," he said, barely audible over the hum of the equipment. "But it might work. If we try it, we'll have to have a clear plan, fully detailed, because we can't afford any other radio contact. Once we separate, each unit will have to know exactly what the others are going to do. The only radio transmissions will be false ones, designed to lure the enemy where we want to be. Let me think about it."

"What about the airplane Major Schevardnadze spotted near the village?" Chertok asked. "Can you explain that?"

"There is only one explanation that makes sense. Our friends have received reinforcements. Nothing else is possible."

"That means we have no time to lose."

Borlov's plan was carefully sketched. As soon as he finished laying it out, the team rushed to execute it.

The Soviet unit split into halves, each taking a separate route. The detailed briefing had covered every conceivable contingency. Borlov took command of one unit, assigning Chertok to lead another. Schevardnadze would accompany Borlov.

The plan was simple, but that was its principal virtue. Even Schevardnadze had been impressed with the economical elegance of the concept. Even before moving out, they had begun to lay the groundwork. A couple of short bursts of radio communication, couched in elliptical language, subtly but nonetheless apparently concealing something significant, were sent out to no one.

Fifteen minutes later they were on the move. One of the APCs stood alone in the gathering darkness. Inside, a makeshift complex of timer, tape recorder and walkie-talkie waited to do its part.

Chertok pushed his unit hard. He followed the same route taken hours earlier by Ermine Two. This time, though, they were expecting to make trouble, not to find it. His team approached to within a thousand meters of the scene of the ambush. Chertok, leading the unit alone on a two-man sled, held up his hand.

Instantly the team divided into two columns and forked to either side of the river. Each column worked its way carefully downriver, deliberately taking a circuitous, difficult route back away from the riverbank.

Chertok checked his watch. If the plan were to work, timing was everything. He looked up at the sky, now dark, and moved his lips in what could have been a prayer. A handset, open to receive, dangled around his neck. Five minutes remained. He pushed his column harder.

The terrain was monotonous. Every hill had begun to look

distressingly like every other. Chertok pulled to the side, waving his column on. While they filed past he scanned a map, folded into a neat, flat packet with the target sector on top. In the near darkness it was difficult to establish a correlation between the flat paper and the rolling hills. As near as he could tell, they had another three kilometers to go, but that was as the crow flies. Their lack of a direct path would add at least another kilometer to that distance.

The dangling handset squawked suddenly. Chertok jerked, the noise catching him off-guard. He bent to look at his watch, his heavy mittens fumbling with the push-button for the internal lamp. It was six o'clock, right on the button.

The content of the message wasn't important. What was essential was that the enemy pick it up. To be sure of that, the message would be repeated several times in the next half hour. If all went according to plan, the pieces would start to fall into place.

Chertok gunned his sled, painstakingly making up lost ground. The sleds were running almost flat out, but his was the only one carrying a single rider. The weight differential was significant enough to let him overtake the others. Five minutes later he was back out front.

They were now four kilometers past the point of the ambush. The handset squawked again. Corporal Grigorev had done a good job simulating panic. Even knowing the message was bogus, Chertok had to struggle against the impulse to respond. He only hoped the other side was as convinced as he was.

The distinctive twin peaks of Lord and Lady Mitchell loomed up out of the darkness. How like the British to have memorialized their class system in topographical features, Chertok thought. The dual peaks were insignificant by any reasonable standards but towered over the surrounding countryside to claim pride of place unopposed. "In the land of the blind the one-eyed man is king," Chertok whispered.

Goosing his sled to get the last ounce of power out of the already straining engine, Chertok pulled ahead of the column. After a flat-out sprint of five hundred meters, he allowed the sled to coast. The engine whined down, its overheated cowling crackling as it cooled.

Chertok looked at his watch again.

It was time.

Lifting the handset to his mouth, he inhaled to calm his nerves, then thumbed the mike open. He never thought he'd find himself wishing to be overheard by the enemy. The last prerecorded transmission crackled in the cold air, right on time.

It was his turn.

CHAPTER 24

"Luke, we got something. They answered."

"Did you get a fix?"

"Not quite. Wait a minute, they're talking again . . . got it."

"How far?"

"Under two miles."

"What'd they say, Conroy?"

"It was pretty garbled . . . I'm not sure."

"Well, guess, dammit!"

"The first one, the one we kept hearing over and over, was asking for a location. The response was a distress call. An APC has broken through the ice. Downriver from here—about a mile, I'd guess. Is that right, Steeples?"

"More or less."

"A sitting duck," Luke said. "How convenient."

"I don't like it," Ben said. "I don't like it at all."

"Why not, Ben?"

"Look. Ever since they didn't respond to the phony transmissions we made, we've been assuming they were wise to us. All of a sudden they start using the frequency again. And they're telling us they're stuck. You're right about one thing, Luke. It's too convenient."

"You may have something, Ben. But it doesn't mean we can't take a look."

"All right. I'll take Mackenzie and Padraic. I think you ought to sprint for the target. If this is a trap, we'll save a lot of time. And if it isn't, I'll let you know."

"Ben, listen to me. If you think this is a set up, I don't want you to engage them. You understand? Check it out, then drop back and keep an eye on them. That's all."

"Understood."

"The rest of us will push on and try to make the pickup. I want to get there ahead of them, and ahead of the new kids on the block, whoever they are. The sooner we get this finished, the sooner we can get Patrick out to a hospital."

Ben zipped his parka. He hefted the Suomi speculatively, looking it over the way a pinch hitter coming up in a tight spot checks his bat for cracks and flat spots. A moment later he was gone.

Stepping out into the darkness, he raised his head. His nostrils flared. The broad nose grew even broader. He smelled snow on the way. The cold, wet scent of heavy weather was inescapable.

Padraic was in the four-man tent, tending to his wounded brother. Ben stooped to slip under the heavy canvas flap. The tall Apache had to duck to keep from scraping the tent with his hood. He couldn't imagine how the McCarthy brothers maneuvered inside the tent without bursting its seams.

Ben dropped to one knee beside the cot. Patrick was heavily wrapped in several blankets. His eyes were closed. Ben touched Padraic on the shoulder. "How's he doing?" he whispered.

"It hurts, but not as much as a Mantovani record." The voice was Patrick's. "What's going on?" He opened his eyes and struggled to sit up. Padraic gently pushed him back down.

"I have to take a little trip. Padraic, Luke wants you to go along."

"Sure thing. I'll be right there. Just give me a minute."

"Okay. I'm going to get Mackenzie. I'll be right back." Ben stepped back into the cold. Mackenzie was huddled around a fire with the others. Ben crunched through the snow. Jason turned as he approached.

"Something up?"

"Yup."

"What do I need?"

"Whatever you can carry."

Roland Johnson stood up. "Can I do anything?"

Ben shook his head. "I think Luke is going to push on to the crash site. Jason, Paddy and I are going to check into a little puzzle we picked up on the radio."

"Want any help?"

"No, we can handle it." He turned to walk back to the tent. He heard Mckenzie right behind him.

The tent flapped open, and Padraic stepped out. He had two Suomis draped over his shoulders. "Thought I'd bring Patty's along, since he won't be using it for a while."

Ben nodded. He led the way to the sleds, clustered behind the tent. He dropped into the bucket seat and waited for the others to follow suit. When all three men had strapped themselves in, Ben told them what they'd be looking for. Without waiting for a response, he started his engine. The brittle slap of the small motor sounded inadequate to its purpose in the huge darkness. When the other two engines joined in, the noise was still pathetically thin.

Ben pulled out with a lurch. The others pulled abreast of him, one on either side. Together the sleds hammered into the night. Ben tumbled thoughts in his mind like the pieces of a puzzle. He was trying to get some perspective on what was happening. Everything seemed transparent, until he looked at it carefully, then the clarity receded. Like a chunk from a jigsaw puzzle, it seemed to fit anyplace he tried until it came time to force it home, then the minute differences resisted his efforts.

He was convinced the transmission was bogus but couldn't justify the position with convincing argument. It was a gut feeling, no more than that. He knew Luke felt the same way. Ahead of them, Soviet soldiers waited in the darkness. How many of them, he didn't know. What they intended to do, he couldn't guess. But they were there. And for the moment that was all he had.

He had a vague idea of what to look for, and a much clearer idea of what to expect. The darkness didn't work against him as much as the Soviets were hoping. He smiled at the thought of his ancestors, themselves at home in the dark. The snow that stretched off to the horizon in every direction was hardly an impediment now.

Finally he slowed his sled to a crawl. Referring to the rough map Calvin had sketched, he put their goal less than a mile away.

The signal, though, if it had been designed to lure them into something, would have emanated from a point somewhere beyond the ambush. He stopped his sled and waited for the others.

"What's up?" Jason Mackenzie asked, coasting to a halt beside Ben. "Did you hear something?"

"No, but I think we better go on foot from here."

McCarthy groaned. "That's a long haul, Ben."

"If we want to get home, we better look sharp," Ben said. He slipped on his snowshoes and gave the sled a shove, sending it down into a shallow depression.

Mackenzie walked his down after slipping into his own snowshoes. Padraic struggled with his pair, and Ben took care of his sled. When he returned, the big Irishman was ready. He stood unsteadily on the frail-looking snowshoes and took a couple of tentative steps.

"Are you sure this is necessary?"

"Are you sure it's not?" Ben shot back. He strode off into the night. Behind him, he could hear McCarthy grumbling to himself as he struggled to follow. Mackenzie, more used to the rigors of the environment, had no difficulty keeping up.

The darkness was both an impediment and an ally. Even if they were walking into an ambush, it would be difficult to see them. Noise was their biggest enemy, something McCarthy was having trouble suppressing.

As they walked, Ben swept the ground ahead for some telltale sign of human presence. When they had covered five hundred yards, he held up a hand. Mackenzie, a few yards behind, noticed it and slogged over. Padraic, bringing up the rear, almost bumped into them.

"What now?" he asked.

Ben shushed him. He dropped to one knee and invited the others to do the same. They formed a tight circle, and Ben leaned in to whisper, "If there's anybody here, we have to be getting close. As near as I can tell from Calvin's map, the signal came from over the next rise."

"Any sign?" McCarthy asked.

"None."

"Maybe they got tired of waiting. Maybe they were never here at all."

"I don't know, maybe so. But think about it. If you were going to lure somebody into a trap, you'd take the long way around to get to your position, wouldn't you? No point in leaving a road map and a welcome mat out."

"What do you think we should do, Ben?"

"I think we should spread out. Padraic, you're having a tough time, so you go straight up the rise. It's the shortest route. Jason and I will take either side, circle around the bottom of the hill, and meet you at the bottom of the slope."

"Got you."

"Whatever you do, be quiet. If they're here, they're expecting us. They'll have as much trouble seeing us as we will seeing them. But sound really travels out here. Don't shoot unless you have no choice. And if they have night scopes, you'll be in deep shit. They'll blow you away before you know what hit you."

Ben looked at each man in turn. "Any questions?"

When none were forthcoming, he stood up. "Let's go, and good luck."

When the others had moved off into the dark, Ben sprinted toward the last hill. There was no cover to speak of, and he decided speed was better than caution. Even with a night scope a moving target was tougher to hit.

Ben felt the ground begin to slope upward, and he cut to the right. The hill loomed ahead, still some distance away. He was moving fast and bent forward to cut down on the target area. Dangling from its loose leather sling, his Suomi slapped against his hip. He reached back to quiet it.

Rounding the side of the hill, he pulled up to listen. The

wind, earlier hardly a whisper, had picked up. It was the only noise he heard. So far, so good.

His breath came in short, sharp gasps. The snow was dry, but it still hampered his movement. He envied the waiting men, if they were out there. It had to be an advantage to sit still and let the enemy come to you. The hill was now a dark shadow on his left. He was moving through a wide notch.

A broad, open area lay directly in front of the hill, not so much a valley as a plain. Three hundred yards away, another hill shot up into the darkness. It was too far away for him to see its crest. Instinctively he knew it was a perfect place to wait. He quickened his pace, ignoring the sharp pain in his side.

A series of low hills on the right afforded him cover. He ducked behind the first and sprinted, his legs pumping as fast as they could. To his heightened senses, the thin, almost metallic slap of the snowshoes sounded like cymbals as he ran. He passed the second low hill, little more than twice his height, and rounded its base. The third flew by, and the fourth and last was just ahead. The tallest of the four, it also had the broadest base. Ben cut inside it, keeping the crest of the tall hill just within his field of vision. Behind it, he knew, rose the twin towers of Lord and Lady Mitchell.

Padraic should be just about at the crest of his own hill. Jason would be somewhere below and to the left. He reached the bottom of the hill and stopped. For a split second he debated whether to climb straight up the front of the hill but knew it was the wrong choice. He started running again, puffing and doing his best to ignore the hot lead in his knees. The hill seemed impossibly wide.

He kicked off his snowshoes and started to slog up the rear of the hill. Dropping down to his stomach, he scanned the ridge line. Off to the right he spotted a mound. It could be an outcropping of rock covered with snow. But it looked unnatural. Its contours were too regular. Ben crawled forward, bringing the Suomi around and cradling it in his forearms.

He knew he might be wasting precious time, but the alternative was more deadly. As he crawled, he kept his eye on the mound. He had gone no more than thirty yards when its outline changed. Etched against the dark sky, its edge was clearly defined.

Ben crawled faster.

A figure stood up. Outlined against the sky, it raised something in its hands. Ben realized instantly what it was. The Cyclopean bulge of the infrared sniper scope disappeared as the rifleman leaned into his target.

Without thinking, Ben swung the Suomi to his shoulder. He got to his knees and squeezed the trigger.

The hammering split open the night. Bright flashes spat from the muzzle, splattering blue and yellow shadows on the snow.

The marksman pitched forward and out of sight.

Shouts echoed in the darkness as Ben rolled to one side. If they had seen his muzzle flash, they'd chew him to pieces if he stayed where he was. He rolled over and over, waiting for the inevitable sear of hot metal.

A mound of snow offered him some cover, and he stopped rolling long enough to catch a glimpse of two shadowy figures plummeting toward him. He swung the Suomi up and, lying on his back, squeezed off a burst. He didn't expect to hit anything, but it should keep them honest.

Someone howled with pain. The thudding feet on the hill stopped.

Ben rolled to his stomach and peered into the night. Shadows swam before his eyes. The exertion of his sprint was taking its toll. Bright lights, phosphene flashes from his oxygen-starved retinas, danced like fireflies.

A soft hiss rasped somewhere up the hill. Ben aimed toward the sound and squeezed. The gun slammed into his shoulder, its recoil dampened by the thick padding of the parka. Ben held his breath. So far there had been no sign of anyone else on the hill. As far as he could tell, it was him and the three men above.

Ben started to crawl to his right, then thought better of it. Something thumped into the snow behind him. Instinctively he burrowed into the crusty snow, covering his head with mittened hands. The dull *whump* of the grenade sounded like distant thunder.

Ben was pinned down. He didn't know whether the remaining gunman had a scope, but he had to assume the worst. Sound would give him away, so he couldn't afford to move. But he couldn't wait all night, either. Sooner or later one of them would have to give in.

Ben started to get to his knees when a sudden movement on the crest of the hill caught his eye. He dived back to his stomach.

The shadow moved stealthily. In its hands another scoped rifle, the prominent bulge of the infrared sight bulky above the slender silhouette of the rifle itself. The umbral marksman raised the rifle, and Ben swung his SMG around.

He brought the muzzle up and squeezed, steeling himself for the impact of the recoil. The soft snick of the trigger vanished in the dark. The gun was empty. A second later the sharp hammer of the sniperscope shattered the silence. The report echoed and died.

The shadow descended the slope cautiously. "Ben, you all right?"

It was McCarthy.

Ben jumped to his feet and sprinted toward the big Irishman. "I never thought I'd be so glad to see somebody." Ben laughed.

McCarthy sank down on his haunches. "Me, either. You have no idea how tired I am. The next time I accept work from your Mr. Simpson, you can bet your ass it'll be in a warm climate . . . and a desk job."

CHAPTER 25

Deadly Force was running like hell.

The sleds jounced over increasingly flatter terrain, mounds of snow poking up in every size and shape. Luke kept trying to shake the image of a snow-covered cemetery, which he imagined would look very much like this. The sleds whined like angry violins, the deep bass of the APC playing an ominous counterpoint.

Luke continued to worry about Ben but knew there was nothing he could do. Ben would have to take care of himself. Radio contact was out of the question. The light seemed to be seeping out of the sky like viscous liquid. He no longer needed the goggles, which flapped uselessly on his chest.

Options, that's what it all came down to, options. He was taking a colossal chance, and he knew it. He knew that you couldn't win without taking a few now and then. He also knew you win some and you lose some. Right now Luke didn't feel much like a winner. With his already minuscule team split into smaller units, he was spreading himself thin.

And now he had his own side to worry about. The last word from Jake—and it would be the last until they either wrapped their hands around the ominously beeping grail or watched some other champion carry it off in triumph—had been distressing. Tompkins might not have given Jake all the details, but what he had said was maddening enough. The CIA was putting its own team in. That accounted for the blip at Old Crow. What Luke couldn't figure is why they did it. If they wanted to help, then they could have joined forces. They were, ostensibly, on the same side.

But Luke also knew enough about the mentality of the clandestine bureaucrat to guess that a shared victory was a defeat. Stiles Moreland was widely perceived to be a buffoon in sharp clothing. The CIA had to be full of bruised egos and bit-chomping cowboys waiting for an opportunity to put it to him. This just might be their best shot. If Luke Simpson and Deadly Force got their tit caught in a wringer, too bad. There was no room for high-profile free-lancers, anyway. That, in a nutshell, was the reasoning. Luke was sure of it. What frightened him was the prospect that there might be an undercurrent of active ill will lacing the stew.

More than a few intelligence professionals resented him. They'd had the field to themselves for so long, they'd gotten used to being the only game in town. They were spoiled, sometimes lazy, and often downright incompetent. Luke flashed to Malcolm Conroy, no doubt turning green in the back of the APC. Useless as tits on a boar. If he represented the best the Company could come up with for this assignment, the U.S. might just as well throw up its hands and surrender. It would save a lot of bloodshed.

"Unless . . ." And Luke immediately stopped himself. What would be the point? Even Moreland couldn't be that easily flummoxed. And Conroy wasn't that good an actor. "Still," Luke mumbled to himself and the wind, "it's something to think about."

He thought for a moment that he might be losing it. The notion of Conroy as a capable time bomb, self-activated when the time was ripe, was too dirty to be credible. On the other hand, from an outfit that wanted to change the world by making a dictator's beard fall out, what wasn't possible? So far the kid had been a bump on a log, nothing more. Calvin was keeping a tight rein on him, but there hadn't been a single indication it was even necessary.

Luke flipped on the single sealed-beam headlight. Running at top speed, he wanted to make sure he didn't hit anything. The light was a risk, but hell, just being there was a risk. And right now, getting there first was paramount. Getting there safe, if it meant tiptoeing, wasn't going to cut it. The snarling engines made enough noise that anybody sitting up ahead would hear them coming, anyway.

The brilliant white tunnel carved by the beam whipped and swerved as the sled bounced over the bumpy ground. Luke was reminded of an amusement park ride he'd loved as a kid, shooting through a giant corrugated tube on a rush of white water, the gurgle and hiss of the torrent a distant roaring in his ears. The night shot by on both sides, little more than a collection of skimpy shadows.

Behind him, the other headlights darted and danced, sometimes stabbed past him, mingling with his own beam like a nightmarish light show in a laser museum. The dual yellow lances of the APC painted the snow a sickly color, and the world looked like it had been stained with orange juice.

Malcolm Conroy had a difficult time keeping his balance in the rocking APC. He watched Calvin Steeples work the controls, steering with great sweeps of his broad shoulders. The wheel was wide and nearly flat in front of him. Leaning forward, he kept his eyes fixed on the narrow port, hoping like hell nobody lost power. The clank of the heavy tread slammed through the armor plate and bounced like a raucous Ping-Pong ball from wall to wall before rattling to the floor.

Casually, almost as an afterthought, he felt in his pocket for the flat black plastic card. Feeling along its edge for the small metal pin, he squeezed. The pin slid home. Now, if only it worked.

"There he is," David Naughton yelled. The sudden green flower blooming on dark gray glass winked steadily back at him. "Damn, how far do you make it, Alderson?"

The man at the controls glanced at the screen. "Five, maybe six miles."

"That much?"

"What do you expect? They had a hell of a head start on us."

"How far to the target?"

"Less than twenty miles. Maybe nineteen."

"Can we beat them?"

"I don't know."

"You're paid to know."

"And you're paid to sit down and hold your water. You want to beat them, stay out of the way."

Naughton ignored the jibe. He dropped into a bucket seat behind Alderson, fanning his fingers in a broad web in his lap. Half of the equation was in evidence. Conroy had delivered. But the other half was more dangerous. So far they hadn't had a clue as to the whereabouts of the Soviet team.

Letting Simpson and his outfit pull the weight had been a calculated risk. It put them in the way of some heat, but it also gave them a better picture. Naughton wondered whether it might not have been better to join Simpson and just walk off with the prize at the end.

But if Simpson didn't sit still for it, then what? The man was a pain in the ass, but he was no fool. And he wouldn't back down from a fight, not with anybody. Maybe especially not with the Central Intelligence Agency.

Naughton had gone over the Company files on Deadly Force and on Luke Simpson in particular. It always helped to know your enemy. That was an axiom of the trade. But Simpson wasn't easy to know. The guy was solid, and he knew his stuff. But he was too damned independent for his own good. That made him unpredictable. There were too many unknowns in this mess already, without factoring Simpson in. But if he'd learned one thing in his twenty-plus years in the Agency, it was that things never got easier.

Part of him even admired Simpson. There had been a time, not nearly as long ago as it now seemed, when he had been the same kind of short-fused, high-energy motherfucker. Bullshit was hip-deep, and he didn't want to wear waders, so he kicked ass and let the bone chips land where they may. But the incomparable weight of reality pressed in on him. It crushed brighter eyes and bushier tails than his.

Either way, David Naughton knew, his best days were behind him. He was too old to hope to succeed Stiles Moreland. He didn't know if he even wanted to. The pragmatist in him had strangled his capacity to dream. Reality, that cold, gray, ugly beast, was the only animal in his zoo. He could feed it or let it starve. But if he took the latter course, and the corpse lay cold and dead on a concrete floor, what would he have left?

And that, he knew, was why he had to beat Luke Simpson to the prize. It wasn't any longer, if it ever had been, about intelligence, national security, defense against the Soviet threat. It was about preserving the illusion of his compromise.

If he could beat Simpson, then he had made the right choice, and Simpson was the fool.

"Just keep thinking that way," he mumbled. "Maybe you'll believe it."

"You say something?" Alderson asked over his shoulder.

"No. Nothing. Nothing at all."

Schevardnadze kept his nose buried in his work. The constant signal lulled him into a state of somnambulism. Wordless and ignored, he watched the twinkling light as if it would vanish if he were to blink at the wrong time. He seemed to be adjusting his personal rhythm to that of the beacon.

Borlov chattered behind him, almost gloating in bubbly anticipation. Convinced that his ploy had worked, there was no holding him. The shock and revulsion Schevardnadze had felt at first had long since been numbed. Borlov was a brute fact for which there was no elegant theory, no dispassionate explanation. He had no choice but to accept the existence, perhaps even the dominance, of the Borlovs of the world.

Schevardnadze was so immersed in thought, he almost missed it. He blinked once, then again. When it didn't go away, he knew it had to be real. He watched it in silence. It blinked. It was real.

Reluctantly he called over his shoulder. "Colonel Borlov, there's something here you should see."

The colonel stalked heavily to the rear of the jouncing vehicle. He kept his balance by leaning on the shoulders of the men he passed, huddled in their seats like schoolboys on a runaway bus.

"What is it, Major?"

"See for yourself. There." He pointed with a mittenless finger. The pulsing blob, small, dim green, like throbbing protoplasm on a microscope slide, disappeared under his fingertip.

"Where?"

"Behind us, approximately two kilometers."

"And it wasn't there before?"

"No, sir."

"So the race is to the swift, after all."

"If so, we're in trouble, Colonel. They're gaining on us."

"We can fix that, Major. Never you mind."

CHAPTER 26

Alderson hunched over his equipment. The infrared sensors were new, and he wasn't comfortable with them. He was getting bleary-eyed watching what he considered one screen too many. When the smoky red blurs appeared, he didn't notice them. He had been watching too hard for too long. When they grew brighter, he didn't want to believe it.

"Mr. Naughton, I got something here, but it shouldn't be where it is. I told you this new equipment was junk."

Naughton shook off his reverie and scrambled to peer over Alderson's shoulder. "Let me have a look."

He leaned in to the screen, as if its images would suddenly crystallize. Alderson was right. There was something there. He was also right that it shouldn't be where it was.

"What do you make of it, Sergeant?"

"I dunno. The beacon Conroy's carrying puts him more than two miles away from his location. As far as I know, not even Luke Simpson has figured out how to be in two places at once."

Naughton bristled. "For chrissake, you talk about the guy like he was a superman or something."

"Credit where it's due, Mr. Naughton. Seems reasonable to me."

"Maybe, but if you sit back and stargaze, your hero is going to steal the pants right off you."

"So, we agree it ain't Simpson. Got any ideas?"

"There's only two choices, Alderson. Either Simpson split his team into two units, or we just ran into Ivan."

"Hobson's choice, isn't it?"

"Maybe not. How fast are they moving?"

"If this equipment is reliable, somewhere around twenty miles per hour."

"Can we do better than that?"

"Yeah, but not much. Maybe, and I repeat, *maybe*, twenty-four, twenty-five. But I don't know for how long, and I don't know whether that's their top speed or their cruising speed."

"We'll find out, won't we."

"Yeah, I guess so."

"Any chance they can spot us?"

"Maybe. If they have something like this gizmo, certainly. If they want to take a look-see with radar, probably. Don't ask what the odds are, 'cause I don't have a clue."

Naughton didn't respond immediately. He turned his back on Alderson and stared out the nearest port of the sleek new M-113 APC. It was a recon model, fitted with two 7.62-mm rapid-fire cannon and sporting a spiffy little item hastily installed by special request: a remote-control turret featuring a pod of Mighty Mouse 2.75-inch rockets, stripped from an Apache assault chopper. It was an ingenious idea, but nobody believed it would work. Nobody but Naughton, who, whatever his shortcomings, would never be accused of lacking self-confidence.

His problem now was an elementary one. Logically there was no reason for Simpson to have split his team. It was too small by half as it was. That left the chilling, but certainly more exhilarating, option: it was the Soviet insertion team, or a substantial part of it, judging by the covey of hot spots on the infrared. There remained therefore only one decision to be made: Should he engage them in combat or simply try to outrun them?

Wisdom dictated restraint. But the cold, hard fact was that the enemy detachment was directly ahead of him. They were two miles closer than he, and the rocket payload was only twenty miles away.

He might outrun them on a straight course, but this wasn't a NASCAR feature. When he caught them, military engagement was a virtual certainty. If he took a longer route to skirt them, he would be ceding an additional advantage to an opponent who already had a lead on him. The decision, therefore, had been made for him. Engagement was the only solution, and it might just as well be on his terms.

"All right," he said, spinning around to lean over Alderson's shoulder again. "Here's what we're going to do. Get Molson and Martinson on the comm laser. I don't want radio communication. We need every edge we can get."

Alderson shook his head, muttering to himself. "Oh, boy, I can hardly wait to hear this." He clicked the switch on the comm laser, locking his laser feed onto the receiver of the second M-113. "Locked on."

Naughton waited anxiously, like a first-time father in the delivery room. He felt like he should be doing something, but for the moment matters were out of his hands. The first order of business was to get in tight. He could lob a Mighty Mouse at this range, but he wanted visual contact. There was still a chance, however slim, that the units ahead were friendly, or at least neutral. At heart he was a gunslinger, but with regular Army along, he had to keep his range-war instincts in check. Molson was in one of the other two APCs. Naughton knew the captain was a book man. No chance of running anything fancy with him around to keep tabs.

Pushing the APCs hard, their big diesel engines rumbling like tectonic plates grinding together, they were closing the gap. Molson questioned the strategy. He pointed out—wisely, Alderson thought—that engagement was a high-risk proposition. They had no idea of the kind of firepower the enemy might be packing.

Naughton shot back that it was the kind of thinking that would have George Patton whirling in his grave like a drunken dervish. Molson responded that Naughton was likely to get a firsthand chance to see just what Patton might be doing, unless they used a little more caution.

And while they debated, the APCs drew still closer to the shimmering subject of the debate. At three thousand yards Alderson sounded the first alert. The undulating terrain made laser sighting unworkable. Straight line-of-sight was a prerequisite for the sophisticated laser sighting to be effective.

Naughton was chafing at the restraints imposed on his itchy trigger finger by technology. What good was all this science-fiction crap? If you had to get that close, you might as well be Captain Kidd boarding a frigate on the high seas. Alderson thought the complaint more in the nature of a wish but bit his tongue on the verge of saying so.

At twenty-five hundred yards, Alderson noticed a sudden change in the pattern of blips.

"I think they've spotted us, Mr. Naughton. They're fanning out."

"What's the terrain up there, Mr. Alderson?"

"They're on the ice. Typical estuarine valley contours."

"In English, Alderson."

"It's a river valley. Low hills on both sides. Broad plane on either bank, then rapid increase in elevation."

"How wide?"

"A thousand yards, give or take."

"And what's their dispersion?"

"Fifty percent to either side. I make it fourteen vehicles. Two large, comparable to ours, and the rest small. Jeeps or smaller. Looks like they're setting up on both banks. Probably climbing the hills."

"Are they running?"

"No, sir. No such luck."

"I guess we don't have to worry about them being friendly, do we?"

"Eighteen hundred yards. They've stopped moving. We're going to close fast. You still want a visual?"

"Hell, no. Let me know when you pick them up on the lasers. And patch this over to Molson and Martinson. I want to kick ass in a hurry."

A soft ping echoed through the M-113's mausoleumlike innards.

"Radar. They spotted us for sure."

"They must be pretty sure of themselves to risk using radar."

"We didn't exactly give them much choice. Fifteen hundred yards. Contact—"

The rest of Naughton's words were drowned out by an earsplitting roar. The APC tilted crazily to one side. It rose as if in the grip of a giant fist, then settled heavily back. It yawed and seemed to spin.

"One track's gone. We're not getting any traction on the left."

"What the hell was that?" Naughton spluttered.

"It was heavy shit, whatever it was. We're dead in the water, Naughton. Let's get the hell out of here. We're sitting ducks."

As if to punctuate the sentence, a second explosion slammed into the APC. A near miss, it rained splinters of hot metal onto the heavy armor plate. Then a steady hail rattled against it. It sounded as if they were being pelted by handfuls of cutlery. The whining ricochets were deafening. The dead-on hits sounded like the blows of a hammer driving nails in a coffin.

"How long do you think we'll last outside?" Naughton asked. Alderson thought his voice cracked, but he didn't blame the man.

"How long do you think we'll last if we aren't?"

"Alderson, this is Molson. Are you all right?"

It was the radio. Molson, realizing radio silence was an unnecessary fiction, was shouting. The crackle of the radio dampened the incessant screech of metal on metal.

"Alderson, hang on, I'm going to drop a little on them."

The dull bass of a heavy cannon opened up. Naughton knew from the proximity that it was Molson. The IR screen showed a flurry of activity. Small blips, like a swarm of hornets, swirled in tight circles. Whatever they were, Alderson realized, they were too busy avoiding Molson's fire to pose any immediate threat. That must mean they were either lightly armored or bereft of plate altogether.

"Sleds! They're sleds!" Alderson was shouting.

"What are you talking about?" Naughton yelled.

"Look at the IR. They have to be sleds. I told you they were small. It has to be. The two big ones are probably APCs. Tell Molson to take the big ones out."

"I heard that," crackled a voice over the radio. "But you guys have the Mighty Mouse. All I've got is the cannon. You'll have to do it yourself."

Alderson clicked the laser sight on. The viewfinder glowed softly, its cross hairs and calibration starkly etched against the glow. The hungry beam, seeking desperately to save its own life, locked on the smallest of targets. Almost totally hidden behind the crest of a hill, it found the right front track and a square yard of sloping armor plate.

He keyed the turret servo, and the whirring sound of the powerful motor saturated the metal room. Canted over on one side, the crippled APC was almost defenseless. The turret swiveled, the servo grinding, trying to improve its angle of fire.

"I don't know if we can get the right angle," Alderson said through clenched teeth.

"We'd better," Naughton said. The edge of desperation raised his voice half an octave.

"Here goes nothing."

CHAPTER 27

The shattering eruption caught Ben by surprise. The sudden flash threw dark shadows across the snow. He had heard the engines but had been unable to see anything. Armed now with the captured sniper rifles, he and Jason Mackenzie roared through a gap in the hills. The location was all wrong for Luke. But something sure as hell was going down.

Padraic McCarthy brought up the rear, the combined weight of the LAW rockets and the big man himself considerably slowing his sled. He saw Ben spin sidewise and kill his engine. The bright flashes, like nearby lightning, plumed up as if the earth had split open and was disgorging all its heat in a continuous display.

By the time Padraic reached the crest of the hill, Ben and Jason had thrown themselves to the snow and were wriggling up the last few yards. McCarthy coasted to a halt just behind them. He sat in the sled with his engine idling.

"What's going on?" he hollered.

Ben turned and put a finger to his lips. The Apache waved him down, and Padraic slid from his sled, walking on his knees to the Indian's side. He slid forward to a supine position and peered over the frozen crust of snow, a translucent lip left behind by the wind. He peered through the snow as if through a makeshift window.

Across a narrow valley, a Soviet APC rocked on its tracks. Its cannon hammered incessantly, the flash of its muzzle like a lightning generator flashing news of the end of the world.

"Who the hell are they shooting at?" McCarthy whispered. Ben could barely hear him over the unrelenting fire. "It can't be any of our boys, can it?"

"Not likely," Ben said. "Maybe whoever landed at Old Crow has caught up to us."

"But if they were on our team, we'd know about it, wouldn't we?"

"Yeah. It's nice to think so, isn't it?" Ben smiled a tight, sardonic smile. "But if you make your living keeping secrets, sometimes you keep one too many."

"What shall we do?"

"Let's take that sucker out," Ben said.

Mackenzie remained silent. He kept seeing Sam Waters, his shirttail flapping like a silent semaphore as he charged up the street with his shotgun in his hand. "Yeah, let's," he said, breaking his silence for the first time. "Paddy, give me a couple of those LAWs."

"You know how to use them?" Ben asked.

"Better than I do this thing." He tossed the IR sniper rifle to McCarthy. "Paddy, I'll trade you."

"What are you going to do?" Ben asked. He was afraid he already knew the answer to that question.

Mackenzie waited until McCarthy yanked the rifle out of the way and handed him two LAW tubes. "If I can get in tight, I can put one right up his ass. He'll never know what hit him."

"We can try to take him down from here."

"And if we miss, he'll just duck over the hill. Then we're right back where we started, except he'll know we're here."

Ben nodded. Mackenzie was right and he knew it. But he didn't like the idea of the Canadian taking the risk. "Why don't you let me do it?"

"Because you are going to have your hands full if I don't take them out completely. They'll come spilling out of there like ants from under a rotten log. The two of you should at least be able to cover me, and maybe do better than that."

"Okay, Jason, but be careful."

"If I'm good, I won't have to be careful."

Mackenzie slung the LAWs over his shoulder and slithered down the front of the hill. The slope was fairly steep, and he made good time. As the firefight continued to light up the air intermittently, Ben watched the Canadian's figure gradually blend in with the ground over which he crawled.

When Mackenzie vanished, Ben hauled the sniper rifle around and positioned himself on the top of the rise. McCarthy lay beside him. "Anything I should know about this bugger, Ben?"

"It practically shoots itself," Ben said. He reached into the pocket of his parka and scooped two handfuls of ammunition for the futuristic-looking rifle into the snow. He packed the snow flat with a few tamps of his mittened fist, then moved the shells to the hollow depression. They were standard 7.62-mm Warsaw Pact rounds, probably with a special load.

A combination flash and sound suppressor gave the rifle a squat, almost snub-nosed appearance. Ben flicked the IR sight on and depressed the battery-check button to make sure the IR image was reliable. The small needle floated in the middle of the normal range, and Ben clicked his teeth in satisfaction. He switched weapons with McCarthy and ran the same check. It, too, was in working order.

"Now we wait," Ben said. His voice was flat, almost toneless, and McCarthy wondered whether it was a composure born of will or if Ben was just naturally emotionless. There was something that smacked of the automaton in the inflectionless delivery.

Ben used the IR scope to look for Mackenzie. It took him a while. Jason had made very good time and was now halfway across the flat floor of the small valley. For some reason the APC had stopped firing. Intermittent rifle fire, crackling over the distant snarl of sled engines whining their frenetic soprano, suggested the engagement had merely fallen into a lull. It was certainly not over.

Ben kept the scope on Jason until he saw the Canadian

swing the first LAW around and extend the firing tube. In the broad, circular view screen of the IR sight, he saw the much-diminished figure of Mackenzie flip the LAW sight up and then get to his knees.

When Mackenzie brought the tube into firing position, Ben switched his aim to the APC. He held his breath, waiting for the deep, hollow *whomp* that would signal the rocket launch.

Before it came, a ball of fire broke open, and the APC disappeared. From the hollow behind the APC, a thunderous roar ballooned up and out. Waves of sound broke over him, and he dropped the rifle.

He was certain Mackenzie hadn't fired. With the naked eye he could just barely make out the shadowy silhouette of the APC. It was tilted at a forty-five degree angle but seemed otherwise unharmed. Whatever happened had torn hell out of the snow on which the APC was sitting, but missed the vehicle.

Ben reached for the rifle and heard the hollow thump of Mackenzie's first LAW as he brought the scope up.

Another thunderball mushroomed, and Ben knew Mackenzie had been right on target. Burning fuel gushed from a ruptured tank, then swallowed the harsh contours of the APC. Everything seemed to be moving at half speed. Ben watched the liquid, still not fully aflame, pour out onto the snow, then the fire caught up to its leading edge. The black, twisted metal looked like an artifact from another time, another war.

The top hatch flew back, and a gray shadow, half hidden by the garish light of its flaming skin, tumbled through and fell into the flaming pool beside the stricken vehicle. Instinctively Ben closed his ears to block out the screams he knew would follow hard on the heels of the fiery vision.

The thundering echo rolled past, then echoed from the low hills surrounding them. As it died, a rumble, like the last snore of a waking giant, spread out over the sudden stillness. A pair of lights stabbed into the night, and a second APC roared into view.

Starkly etched in the twin beams, Jason Mackenzie got to his feet. He struggled back a few steps, swinging the tube of the second LAW around to his shoulder. He dropped back to one knee.

Liquid fire lanced out of the advancing behemoth, and the rattle of a .50-caliber machine gun, spitting tracers, crackled over the baritone rumble.

Mackenzie went down, falling over backward in the snow. His finger closed over the trigger of the LAW, and the unguided rocket speared up and away, trailing a plume of thin gray smoke behind it. A moment later it was gone. The APC continued to advance, the trajectory of its tracer fire growing shorter, its angle more acute.

The awful clanking of its tread seemed inexorable, and then it was gone. The whining sleds seemed to recover their composure, and they swarmed off to the left, leaving only a thin echo of sound, as ghostly as the rocket's filament of smoke behind.

McCarthy was the first to recover. He grabbed a LAW from the sled behind him and ran down the front of the hill. Ben called after him to come back, but McCarthy lumbered on, waving the pathetic wand after a lumbering monster he could no longer see.

Ben jumped to his sled, tossed the sniper rifles into McCarthy's, and started his engine. He grabbed the short tether dangling from the Irishman's sled and lurched over the hill and down.

In the pale finger of light cast by his single headlamp, the blocky man's gait seemed comical, rather like a faerie dancing in the moonlight. Ben sped straight for the spot he'd last seen Mackenzie. He was certain the APC had run right over him, but a part of him still hoped the tracks had passed on either side of the prostrate man. Even as he careened down the hill, he knew it didn't matter. There was no way he had survived that murderous fire from the .50-caliber MG. Miracles were just in too damn short supply.

The sled bottomed out, and Ben strained his eyes. In the distance he could hear the last vestigial sounds of the fleeing sleds. The deeper rumble of the APC had long since dwindled away. A dark clump of shadow lay at the center of the valley floor. Ben stopped his sled a few yards short of the shadowy depression. He let go of the tether and got to his feet.

Mackenzie lay on his back. His chest was covered with blood. The LAW tube lay just beyond the straining fingers of one outstretched arm.

On either side of Mackenzie, deep depressions made by the APC tracks seemed to outline the body, as if to emphasize the permanence, the significance, of his death. Ben knelt by the fallen man. Knowing it was futile, he reached out to take one bare wrist in his hand.

He tucked his own hand under one arm and slid the hand out of its mitten. He closed his shaking fingers over the wrist. The skin was cold, the coldest thing Ben had ever felt in his life. An involuntary shudder started at the base of his spine and sped up to explode between his shoulders.

Mackenzie's eyes were open. He was staring at the sky. The vague, empty look seemed more one of expectation than of wonder. Instinctively Ben followed their lead. He tilted his head toward the sky. Behind him he heard the wind rising. Small white specks danced against the dark gray background. Snow began to fall, the first landing on Ben's upturned cheeks. They felt warm as they melted, running down his cheeks. And then he realized they were tears.

McCarthy came back to stand beside the kneeling Indian. He placed one huge hand on Ben's shoulders, then tugged him to his feet. He pushed Ben gently toward his sled, then knelt, himself, to pick Mackenzie up as easily as if he were a broken doll full of nothing more substantial than straw. He placed the dead man gently down on his own sled, then walked back up the hill without a word.

A moment later Ben heard the angry rasp of the starter. The headlight stabbed through the dark, angled up as if trying to find that same thing Mackenzie had been looking for. The sled bounced over the ridge and slid hissingly over the snow.

McCarthy got out of the sled. He uncoiled a rope and tied it to a D-ring on the front of the sled on which Mackenzie lay. He buckled the dead man into his seat, then said, more to the night than to Ben, "We can't just leave him here."

Ben said nothing.

McCarthy walked back to his own sled and sat down. He buckled himself in. He gunned the engine, the sled lurched forward, and he turned in the direction the APC had taken. The line whipped taut, bowed once and hummed, spattering crystalline snow in every direction, then went stiff as the weight of its cargo asserted itself.

Ben watched him go. His hands sat numbly on the steering wheel. His foot toyed with the gas for a moment, then he popped the clutch and roared into the night. McCarthy sat stiffly, outlined in the headlight beam. The dismal trailer bobbed lazily behind, as if it were empty.

In a way, Ben thought, it is.

CHAPTER 28

"Four miles."

"Where's the Soviet unit, Cal?"

"I make it three thousand yards behind us. But they're not closing the gap."

"Not good enough. We won't have time to make a pickup. We don't even know how big the damn thing is."

"What do you want to do?"

"It's not what I want, it's what I have to do. I'm going to stay here and throw the biggest monkey wrench I can find into the works."

"How much help you gonna need?"

"Only as much as I have, I hope."

"You a practical dude, ain't you, Luke?"

"Yeah, I am that, buddy. Pick a spot to drop me. I want to huddle while I diagram the play. Then you run the post pattern while I block."

"That's what I like about you white boys. You know where the speed is, and you ain't too small to admit it. Dr. King'd be right proud."

"You're too humble by half, Calvin."

"Here's as good a place as any. Don't take too long.

They've been pinging away with that damn radar. They know we're here. As long as we keep moving, we'll be all right. But they do like a sitting duck.''

Steeples shifted down. The changing gears ground with the infernal racket of tectonic plates. The lurching M-113 caught the eye of the rest of the men, riding shotgun on sleds. Roland Johnson skidded to a halt just under the rumbling engine. Exhaust clouds swirled around him as he unbelted. By the time he was free of the restraint, the hatch had opened and Luke was dropping to the snow. Calvin followed him down. Conroy stuck his head out but made no move to leave the APC.

Rick Silverbird left his own sled to join the two men. "The buck stops here, eh?"

"White folks don't call us 'bucks' no more," Calvin said to the tall Indian. He wasn't smiling.

"Apparently you don't know much about the Indian Wars, either," Rick said.

"Oh, yeah, right. I forgot. Some insults are universal, ain't they?"

"Forget it."

"Come on, you guys, we can solve the race problem later," Luke barked. "Listen up! Cal, take the APC, Conroy, and Patty. Roland, Rick, and I will stay here and run interference. Whatever you hear, whatever you see on the screen, don't stop. You get to that payload. If you can salvage it whole, do it. Then get Mickey in here for the pickup. If you can't, think of something. We'll stop them if we can, but if they get past us, I want to make damn sure they don't get it back."

"What do you need, Luke?"

"Anything that isn't nailed, bolted, or welded down."

"You got it." Calvin climbed back into the APC. Johnson climbed up and leaned down into the hatch. He passed a dozen LAW rockets, three at a time, down to Luke, who stacked them on one sled. Two boxes of ammo for the Suomis followed, along with an M-79 grenade launcher and a crate of grenades.

"That's about it for the fireworks, boss."

"If wishes were horses . . ." Luke said. He didn't have to finish the quote. "All right, Calvin, get moving. And Conroy, you give him any trouble, he'll kill you. You understand me?"

Conroy swallowed thickly. "Yeah."

"Look, I know you're the reason your buddies were able to find us. Whatever it is you're carrying, ditch it right now."

"I don't know what you're talking about. I—"

"Cut the shit. If you want to run the rest of the way in your birthday suit, I guess you can. And that's what you'll do unless you give me the beacon, pronto. I don't have time to search you, so make up your mind."

Conroy made no move. Luke shook his head slowly. "Okay, if that's the way you want it. Cal, help Mr. Conroy out of his clothes, would you?"

"You're joking." Conroy didn't sound as if he believed what he said.

"Try me."

Steeples stepped forward and looped a thick forearm around Conroy's neck. With his free hand he started unfastening the parka.

"All right, all right. Wait a minute." Conroy slid a hand into his coat pocket. He handed Luke a flat plastic wafer, apparently an American Express Card. On closer examination it proved to be slightly thicker than usual.

"That's it?" Luke sound unconvinced.

"That's it, I swear."

"Show me."

Conroy removed a mitten and indicated the small pin insert.

"What happens if I pull this doohickey out?" Calvin asked.

"Nothing. It activates the electronics, but it's a one-time-only switch. You can't shut it off."

"Then I guess I'll take it with me," Luke said. "If I don't catch up to you, you can always find me. Besides, I never leave home without one of these." Luke slipped the beacon into his pocket. "Let's roll. And watch your ass, Cal. I don't know whether we can hold off the home team as well as the visitors."

Calvin shook his head slowly. "I'll see you soon, okay?"

He climbed up to the deck of the M-113, then reached down to grab Conroy by the collar. He hauled him up bodily, then followed Conroy into the APC. The engine rumbled, and a minute later it was gone.

"Now what?" Silverbird asked.

"Time we put up decorations for the prom, don't you think?"

The whine of the sleds grew louder. Luke felt a visceral pull. The urge to move, to do something, anything, was almost overwhelming. The last thing he wanted to do was to stay put. Rick was wriggling in the snow beside him, as if he, too, found immobility unbearable. The whine became a snarl. The approaching sound increased in pitch. Doppler had it right; he just didn't calculate its effect on blood pressure.

Luke moved the M-79 grenade launcher around to his side. It felt good just hefting the bulky weapon. Burning off a little nervous energy focused Luke's attention. He inhaled, held it thirty seconds, then let it out in a long, slow, sinuous skein of smoky breath.

The sleds were wound tight. It might mean the Soviets were so intent on getting there firstest with the mostest, they might get sloppy. Careless wasn't as good as reckless, but Luke would take what he could get.

"Simpson, you say the word," Roland whispered. He was talking just to let off steam, and all three of them knew it.

The sleds came closer, and the pressure of their imminent presence was almost palpable. It pushed against the three men like a hard, invisible wall. Luke fancied he could reach out and feel it, press his palm flat, and watch his fingertips grow white with the contact.

The first beam of light speared up and over the hill in front of them. It looped awkwardly then, like a rock falling off the edge of a table, slammed down. The slap of the sled's runners on the hard snow was audible under the oscillating hum of its laboring engine. Two more lights speared over the hill, froze momentarily, then plunged out and down. Roland started to move, and Luke grabbed him by the coattail.

"Wait a minute. We don't want to overplay our hand. Let them come to us."

"Come, hell, man. They're already here."

"Not all of them. Listen."

Luke held up a hand for silence. The three sleds were below them, almost abreast of one another. The racket was slicing through the air like shards of broken glass. Swirling snow danced in the headlamps. Each flake seemed to pursue its own course, ignoring both gravity and wind to spiral up and away, then dart with the contradictory grace of a hummingbird.

Luke flipped his parka hood back away from his ears. The wind was a slow, steady moan, white noise in a white wilderness. The engines, clamoring for attention, drowned it out without half trying. And then, just when Luke was about to concede Roland's point, another pair lanced over the hill. Immediately behind them, running hot and sluggish, was a Soviet APC. One of the sleds made a wide loop and bored in toward the armor for a moment. The distinctive CCCP logo, in red and gold, leapt out at him off the mottled white side of the APC.

"Thar she blows, Cap'n," Roland hollered. "What say ye?"

"Let the good times roll."

"All right!"

"Make sure we take the APC first, guys. If we get that baby, the sleds are just about useless. They can't lug anything out of here on them."

"You got it."

Luke drew a bead on the armor with the grenade launcher. The jouncing monster presented a tough target. Its driver was swerving back and forth, doing his best to avoid the larger humps and mounds of snow. It couldn't have been more effective if it had been deliberate evasive action.

"Come on, you bastard. Hold it steady." Luke whispered through clenched teeth.

For a second it seemed as if the driver must have heard him. The APC nosed down, its tracks throwing great gouts of snow behind them as it lost traction for a second. Luke zeroed in and squeezed. He felt the recoil at the same instant the tracks bit and caught hold.

The APC lurched, its nose climbing, and the grenade sailed high, just grazing the rear plate as the ass end dipped down. It clanged once and blew by. The detonation, almost harmless, fountained snow into the air behind and to the right.

The buzzing sleds stopped, as if stunned. The two closest to the armor circled back. For a second Luke thought they'd been spotted, but the sleds continued on, circled around the APC, and fell in behind it.

Roland uncorked a LAW, and the rocket homed in, catching the APC low and to the rear. The earsplitting crack of the charge was swallowed by a ball of flame. The flame, in turn, vanished into a smoky cloud. A series of clanks and sprongs, like the uncoiling of a giant spring, echoed across the flat.

When the smoke cleared, the armor's right track lay flat, sheared off by the blast. It lay useless, a segmented bridge to nowhere.

"Now we're talking!" Roland hollered.

One of the two sleds lay on its side, its engine still droning. Luke let fly with a second grenade, and the sled disappeared in a cloud of smoke and snow. A metallic hum emanated from the gouted cloud. Luke recognized the buzz-saw whine of a turret servo.

"Hit the deck!"

He dived to the left, dragging Roland down below the crest of the hill. Something clawed at the snowline on the ridge, and a staccato drumming followed hard on its heels. The faster-than-sound cannon fire belatedly introduced itself.

Luke tapped Roland on the shoulder to get his attention. It was pointless to try to make himself heard. Instead he tilted his head to the right, tucked the grenade launcher in tight to his body, and rolled. Roland grabbed a brace of LAWs and followed him.

The cannon stopped abruptly. The silence that followed was louder than anything they had so far heard.

"Maybe he's out of ammo," Roland suggested.

"No way. The ammo drums on those babies hold thousands of rounds. Either he thinks he got us, or he wants to see what we do now.''

"What are we going to do?"

"You and Rick stay here. Keep an eye on him. You see anything hop out of the turret, or one of those sleds coming this way, burn hell out of him with the SMGs.''

"What about you?"

"I'm going to move in a little closer and get rid of those LAWs.''

"Right, they just weighing me down, anyhow. Kind of cramp my style, you know? In fact, if you don't mind, I just as soon deliver 'em myself. Always wanted to be a mailman.''

Luke didn't answer immediately.

"Time's a-wasting, Luke. What do you say?"

"Okay. But watch yourself. You see anything moving out there, get your ass back here on the double.''

"Don't worry about me, man. I been takin' care a myself a long, long time.''

Johnson got to his feet. Bent double, the awkward snow-shoes flapping like clown shoes, he looked like a Martian Groucho Marx. All he needed was a cigar and bushy eyebrows. Luke watched him go, then he and Rick slid up to the ridge again, keeping a low profile. If the turret gunner spotted them, they'd have to take a dive, and Roland would be hung out to dry.

The night split open behind them, and Luke turned to see the other three sleds roaring right up the hill toward him. He swung the M-79 around and cut loose with a grenade, aiming short to make sure he didn't overshoot.

The grenade slammed into the cowling of the middle sled. It turned the slope too broad orange daylight for an instant. The blast took out the left sled as well. The third, on the right, was farther behind. It speared through the smoke and whirling debris.

The gunner opened up with a .30 caliber machine gun. The slugs, every tenth one a tracer, walked up the hill, and Luke dived to the left, rolling down to stay out of the cone of illumination thrown by the headlight. His sudden dive caused the driver to swerve, and the gunner lost control, spearing tracers up over the hill and on into the night sky.

Regaining his balance, the gunner had lost his target. He fired blind. A sharp crack from off to the right took out the headlamp. Another report, and then a third, followed. The sled veered wildly left, then seemed to skid sidewise, a pinwheeling shadow out of control in the swirling snow.

Rick fired again, this time using the Suomi, and the whining ricochets testified to his accuracy.

The sled engine sputtered, and a small cone of orange and blue flame, like the tip of a welder's torch, shot out, instantaneously expanding to enormous proportions. Only then did Luke hear the noise as the sled's fuel tank blew.

Luke burrowed into the snow as debris rained all around him. The side of the hill was dark again, and silent. He got to his knees and called to Rick.

"You okay?"

"Yeah, I think so."

"Where are—" The rest of his question was drowned out by the enormous roar rolling up over the hill behind him. Roland had made a special delivery.

And now there was nobody home.

CHAPTER 29

"Two thousand yards. Man, I can almost hear that thing without the scanner." Calvin was ecstatic. "I guess we're gonna take the prize, after all."

"Don't count your chickens, boyo," Patrick hollered from the cot. "And try to skip some of the bigger bumps, if you please. I'm still feeling a little woozy."

"Big man, we're all gonna be woozy when we lay our hands on that baby."

"We haven't found it yet, you know."

"We will, Patty, you can bet the Blarney Stone on that."

"Shame on you, lad. You're committin' a blasphemy, now. For shame."

"I'm not Irish, Patty, so it's not a sin. Fifteen hundred yards. Less than a mile! Man, is Luke ever going to be happy. You can bet your ass we get a bonus this time."

Conroy remained silent, curiously unaffected by the party mood bubbling up in his colleagues. He sat glumly in his bucket seat, his hands folded in his lap.

"Buck up, boyo," Patty said. "Even the CIA can't win them all."

Conroy ignored him.

"Forget it, Patty. Them spooks got no sense of humor, anyhow. One thousand yards."

Steeples leaned forward, keeping one eye on the scanner screen and one on the view port. The terrain was half hidden by swirling snow, but even the horrendous visibilty couldn't dampen his spirits.

"Nine hundred yards . . . eight hundred . . . seven hundred . . ."

Patty McCarthy listened intently, like a kid hearing a fairy tale for the first time, as if he were trying to visualize their quarry in his mind's eye. His mouth hung open in anticipation.

"Six hundred . . ."

"Can you see anything, Calvin?"

"Not yet. But we're gettin' close now, man."

"Well, don't be runnin' it over, man."

"You can forget that. I didn't come all this way to make no pile of junk out of it. Five hundred yards."

Conroy stared at his lap. He might have been sleeping, for all the involvement he exhibited in the quest. He yawned once, looked around the steel container in which he rode, then closed his eyes. He covered his mouth with his hand, the absent gesture of a bored student in history class.

"Four hundred yards . . ."

"Give a holler as soon as you see something, Calvin, there's a good man. I want to get up and see it." McCarthy unlaced the straps holding him on the cot. His arm was throbbing, but for the first time since he had been wounded, he was able to think about something else. He left the strap across his thighs and sat up, bracing himself against the wall of the APC with his good arm.

The wounded arm was strapped tightly to his chest with an Ace bandage. He couldn't move it if he wanted to. He shook his head to sweep aside some of the cobwebs. The painkillers he'd been eating like candy had dulled his senses, even though they hadn't put him to sleep.

"Three hundred . . ."

Conroy opened his eyes and stared at the Irishman as if seeing him for the first time. His mouth opened, and Patty thought he was going to say something, but then the jaw snapped shut and Conroy turned away.

"Two hundred yards . . . one-fifty . . . one hundred . . ."

"You better slow down, man, you'll run right past it."

Steeples geared down, jerking the APC awkwardly as he speed-shifted. The engine roared while the clutch was disengaged, then settled down to a quiet thunder. The rumble filled the tight confines of the APC, pressing on the men's eardrums and raising their blood pressure a dozen points.

"Seventy-five . . . fifty . . ."

"Nothing yet, Calvin?"

"Can't see shit, man. It's snowing like a bitch out there."

"Don't you worry, we'll find it. It's just a matter of time now."

"You forget, man," Calvin grunted, dropping down another gear. "Time's the one thing we ain't got."

"All in due course, boyo."

"Twenty-five yards . . . and . . . I think it's time to pull over. We here, wherever here is. . . ." He threw the big diesels into neutral and left them running. He turned up the gain on the scanner, and the beep of the beacon was deafening. "Hear that? That's the sound of El Dorado, the Fountain of Youth, and the Holy Grail all rolled into one, babe. Pay dirt!"

He reached up to throw back the hatch.

Pat McCarthy unlashed his legs and swung them over the edge of the cot. He grabbed his parka from the floor and struggled into it, fastening the front clumsily, with one arm inside the heavy coat.

Steeples climbed through the hatch, and his feet rapped on the heavy plate as he ran forward and leapt into the snow. McCarthy struggled up the ladder and sat on the deck, swinging his legs out one at a time.

"See anything, Calvin?"

"Yeah, snow, lots of it!"

He ran ahead, kicking at clumps of snow with his heavy boots. Without snowshoes the going was heavy. Several mounds of snow betrayed the presence of something underneath. Steeples kicked at a few, powdering the crust but striking nothing.

A few yards farther on, he caught the glint of something alien projecting up through the crust. It glittered in the bright glow of the headlamps, even through the snow swirling in small clouds just above the surface.

"Here's something. It's metal." He grabbed the flat, jagged-edged projecting with one mittened hand. Bending over it, he scraped away clinging snow with the other hand. "I don't know what it is, but it ain't no Eskimo artifact, I can tell you that."

McCarthy struggled after him and veered off to the left. A mound, larger than the others, had caught his eye. Just out of the glow of the headlamps, it seemed unnaturally flat on top. He kicked at the snow, then fell to one knee and used his one good arm to sweep the dry, dusty snow aside.

"Begorrah!"

"What've you got?"

"Damned if I know, boyo, but it's got writing on it. And if I know my alien alphabets, 'tis neither Greek nor Arabic."

Calvin leapt through the snow to join him. McCarthy stood back while he plowed at the snow with one foot, gouging a ditch along the side of the mound.

"This is it! I swear to God, this is it! It's got to be. This sucker must be twelve feet long. It's sunk in the ground too. I don't know how big it is, but this has to be it!"

He continued to sweep away the snow, revealing a cylinder of polished metal. It was badly dented on the exposed surface, but there was no question it was intact. He scraped away at a small plate set in the side of the cylinder. It was smooth and seamlessly attached. The bright red lettering, three paragraphs' worth, were undoubtedly Russian. "Where's Conroy? He can read this shit. Conroy? Conroy?"

"No need to shout, Mr. Steeples."

Calvin turned to find himself staring into the rather large, and certainly ugly, muzzle of a .45-caliber Colt automatic.

"What the hell are you doing? Put that damn gun down, Conroy, and tell me what this says."

"In due course."

"What are you, crazy? What the hell you think you're gonna do, carry this sucker back to Langley by yourself?"

"No need to do that. I'll have plenty of help in a while. Why don't we just go back inside where it's warm?"

"Why don't you go fuck yourself?"

"Calvin, I think the spalpeen's a wee tad distressed. It might be wise to do what he says."

"He'll be more than a wee tad distressed, I get my hands on him."

McCarthy pushed Calvin ahead of him, leaning on the smaller man for support as they walked back to the APC. Steeples climbed up to the deck, and Conroy waved his pistol, indicating he should go on inside.

"And don't try anything, Mr. Steeples. I won't hesitate to shoot Mr. McCarthy if I have to."

"You really off the deep end, you know that?" Steeples glanced at the young man. The dispassionate, expressionless face spoke volumes. Steeples shook his head and dropped through the hatch.

McCarthy followed, and Conroy climbed in last.

"How you expect your friends to find you? Luke took your little beeper with him."

"You think I only had one? Suppose the battery had failed? Suppose I lost it? I had to have a backup. As it happens, I needed it, didn't I?" Conroy smiled vacantly.

They sat in the close quarters, staring silently at one another. Conroy kept his distance, from time to time glancing at his watch, which was glowing dully in the darkness.

The distant sound of a heavy engine working hard drifted to them on the wind, sifting down through the partially open hatch. Conroy stood up, checked his watch again, and moved over to the hatch. He climbed up the ladder and pushed the hatch all the way open.

He kept the gun trained on them while he poked his head out into the air. "Shit!"

Conroy dropped to the floor of the APC. The engine grew louder, a steady rumble punctuated by the clanking of heavy tread. "It's not ours!"

"What?" Steeples got to his feet.

"It's Russian! What the fuck happened?"

"A little late to worry about that, isn't it?"

Conroy didn't answer. He looked at his watch as if it could explain what had gone wrong. "What'll we do?"

"Your show, babe."

The approaching vehicle stopped. Its engines idled roughly, the broken rumble coming to them as if in fragments as the wind ripped the sound to pieces and scattered them at random.

A turret whined, and Calvin jumped for the ladder. "They're gonna blow our asses to hell. We have to get out of here. He started up the ladder but ducked back down as a burst of machine-gun fire clattered on the heavy armor.

"Do something, Steeples!" Conroy was losing it.

Calvin snatched up the walkie-talkie Ben had captured and shoved it into Conroy's hands. "Talk to 'em, man."

"What'll I tell them?"

"Shit, tell them to give up, we got them surrounded. I don't know. Just keep them busy."

Conroy looked dumbly at the handset. Calvin thumbed it open and gave Conroy a poke with his elbow. "Go on, man," he whispered.

The young CIA man cleared his throat, then spoke rapidly, almost breathlessly. He stopped to listen, and the guttural response crackled loudly in the tight quarters.

"What you tell 'em?" Calvin whispered.

"I told them they were violating international law."

"What'd they say to that?"

"They told me not to interfere. They were here to recover something that belonged to them, and that as long as I butt out, everything will be okay."

"I don't get it," Steeples said. "They been blowing the hell out of anything that moves. Why not us?"

"Maybe they can't?"

"Maybe they—" Steeples stopped as something scraped on the outside of the APC. "What was that? Close the fucking hatch!"

A sharp clatter, then a rattle skittered down the ladder.

"Grenade!"

Steeples shoved Conroy out of the way, and McCarthy grabbed the grenade with his one good hand. He flipped it up and out, then dived away from the hatch. A dull crump rocked the APC.

Calvin sprang up the ladder and grabbed the hatch, hauling it back and down with a clang. He screwed it shut and heaved a sigh of relief.

"That answers that!"

"What do you mean?"

"The machine gun is all they got. They wouldn't have tried the grenade if they had anything heavier."

"What about us? Can we hit them with anything?"

"We're in the same boat. The mini-gun is all we got, and it won't do shit to heavy armor."

"Now what?"

"Mexican standoff."

"Corporal Stepanchev."

"Colonel?"

"Here, take this. I want you to attach it to the capsule."

"What is it, Colonel?"

"Never mind. Just do it."

Chertok spoke so quietly, Schevardnadze wasn't even sure he'd heard him at first. "Those are explosives, Corporal. Colonel Borlov wants to destroy the rocket payload. Isn't that right, Colonel?"

"Of course! It's apparent we won't be able to recover it. My orders were to recover it if possible, but at all costs to make certain that it doesn't fall into American hands."

Borlov drew his pistol and brandished it at the young man. "Now, Corporal!"

"Stay where you are, Stepanchev." Chertok was pointing his own pistol at Borlov.

"Are you insane, Captain Chertok? This is treason."

"Maybe, but it's preferable to madness."

"Corporal, if you disobey my order, you'll regret it. Lubyanka will seem like heaven compared to where you'll end up."

"Colonel, put down your pistol, please." Chertok's voice was preternaturally calm. He stared at Borlov, watching for the least sign of movement.

Borlov spun around, and Chertok fired. The report of the pistol was deafening in the confined space.

Borlov fell to the floor. Chertok stepped toward him and leaned over the fallen man. He brought the pistol down and placed the muzzle flush against Borlov's forehead. "You are extinct, a dinosaur, and you don't even know it," Chertok whispered.

The second report of the pistol was quiet, as casual as an afterthought tossed over the shoulder.

"Major Schevardnadze, contact the Americans again. Tell them we surrender."

EPILOGUE

Luke Simpson still felt cold. Home for more than a week, he had been unable to shake the chill from his bones. He had just finished his final report. Getting to his feet, he walked to the sliding glass door and pushed it open. The desert heat rushed in, and Luke smiled.

Stepping out onto the patio, he dropped into a chair beside Jake O'Bannion. "Beautiful day, isn't it, Jake?"

"Looks like snow to me, Luke."

"You're too old to be such a wise guy, Jake."

"Are you kidding? I'm too old to be anything else. All finished?"

"Yup."

"Bet that's a relief."

"You said it."

"What's going to happen to Chertok?"

"After the Langley boys are done debriefing him, he'll get a new name and a no-show job someplace. He'll be fine. Schevardnadze and the others are already home."

"Strange bird, that Chertok."

"It takes all kinds."

"I still don't know what to make of it all, though. I mean, why'd he do it?"

"Something tells me it wasn't his idea."

"Whose, then?"

"We'll never know. My guess is somebody in the Kremlin. That laser satellite was almost certain to reescalate the arms race. They can't afford it, and neither can we. According to Chertok, the bird was knocked down on purpose. If it wasn't destroyed, we were supposed to get our hands on it. Chertok was sent along to see that we did. Their version of SDI, I guess, and it was a beaut. It would kill anything we had up there."

Jake stood up. Calvin Steeples stood in the doorway. "How are you feeling, lad?"

"I been better. Still feel cold." He walked over to the railing and looked down at the desert spread out below for as far as the eye could see. Slowly, almost languorously, he stretched his arms over his head. Suddenly he looked up at the sky and fluttered his hands.

"What the hell are you doing, Calvin?"

"Cheeese! I'm waving to Tran. You never know who or what is watching you these days. But it's a cinch that little bastard is."

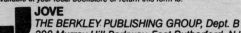